MiLLiONAiRES FOR THE MONTH

Also by Stacy McAnulty

STACY MCANULTY

MILLIONAIRES FOR THE MONTH

RANDOM HOUSE 🏠 NEW YORK

Text copyright © 2020 by Stacy McAnulty
Jacket art copyright © 2020 by Andy Smith

Random House and the colophon are registered trademarks of Penguin Random House LLC.

Visit us on the Web! rhcbooks.com

Educators and librarians, for a variety of teaching tools, visit us at RHTeachersLibrarians.com

Library of Congress Cataloging-in-Publication Data
Names: McAnulty, Stacy, author.
Title: Millionaires for the month / Stacy McAnulty.
Description: First edition. | New York : Random House, 2020. | Audience: Ages 8–12. |
Summary: "After seventh graders Benji and Felix 'borrow' $20 from a lost wallet, the billionaire owner challenges them to spend over $5 million dollars in thirty days in order to learn life lessons about money." —Provided by publisher.
Identifiers: LCCN 2020001662 (print) | LCCN 2020001663 (ebook) |
ISBN 978-0-593-17525-5 (hardcover) | ISBN 978-0-593-17526-2 (library binding) |
ISBN 978-0-593-17527-9 (ebook)
Subjects: CYAC: Money—Fiction. | Wealth—Fiction.
Classification: LCC PZ7.M47825255 Mi 2020 (print) | LCC PZ7.M47825255 (ebook) |
DDC [Fic]—dc23

The text of this book was set in 11.6 pt Archer Book.
Interior design by Cathy Bobak

Printed in the United States of America
10 9 8 7 6 5 4 3 2 1
First Edition

For Henry,
my third novel for my third (and favorite?) kid

MilliONAiRES
FOR THE MONTH

Chapter $1

TUESDAY, OCTOBER 26

Felix Rannells

The seventh-grade teachers of Stirling Middle School did not put any thought into the important task of assigning field trip partners. Their poor decision-making had tethered Felix Rannells to Benji Porter for the entire day. When Felix received his assignment at 6:00 a.m., he considered faking an illness—something tough to prove, like a toothache—but his mom had already driven off. And the field trip was to the American Museum of Natural History in New York City, a place he'd always wanted to go.

So instead, Felix climbed the bus steps and took the inside seat next to Benji. Felix tried to pass the two hours by reading, while Benji tried to entertain everyone by offering to do stupid tricks for money.

"For a dollar, I'll eat gum from the bottom of the seat."

"For a quarter, you can draw on my back with a Sharpie."

"For ten dollars, I'll moon that tractor-trailer."

Benji wasn't making much. He earned a buck off Aidan Rozman and a lot of *ews* from everyone else.

Ideally, Felix should have been paired with someone who respected rules, like a teacher. Or better yet, no partner at all. He liked to be alone, or maybe he was just used to it. Was there really any difference?

Benji and Felix knew each other, of course. They were in Ms. Chenoweth's homeroom, and they both played basketball—Felix, a point guard, and Benji, a center. Benji's nickname on the court was Barney (not that Felix would ever call him that) because he was the biggest guy out there, and he was always smiling. Benji had wavy brown hair, braces, and zits and would probably grow a mustache before they were out of middle school. And like the purple dinosaur, Benji was kind of awkward.

"Hey, buddy." Benji turned to Felix. "I'll give *you* a dollar if you call Ms. Chenoweth 'Mommy' for the rest of the day."

Felix shook his head, regretting again not pretending to be sick when he'd had the chance. Now it was too late.

The bus pulled up in front of the museum, and the students were reminded to stay with their partners at all times. This resulted in Felix spending the morning as an unwilling participant in a three-hour game of hide-and-seek where he was always the seeker. Benji "accidentally" joined another school's group. He went into the bathroom—without permission. He even set off an alarm when he tried to duck behind a woolly mammoth. And approximately every thirty seconds, Ms. Chenoweth warned Benji (and by association, Felix) to behave.

By lunch, Felix needed air and a break. Ms. Chenoweth seemed to read his mind, allowing them all to eat across the street in Central Park. *The* Central Park—as seen in movies.

A chaperone handed out the bagged lunches everyone had prepacked. Felix's contained a peanut butter sandwich and saltine crackers. His mom wouldn't be going to the grocery store again until the end of the month, so they were out of chips and granola bars. He unwrapped the sandwich and ate the larger half in a matter of seconds.

But Benji didn't have a bagged lunch in the cooler. "I forgot it on the counter."

Felix offered him his crackers.

"Nah. I'm buying a pretzel." Benji pulled a wrinkled dollar from his jeans and headed toward a food cart.

You're not supposed to, Felix thought. The permission slip had clearly stated that students were forbidden to make any purchases.

Felix glanced back at Ms. Chenoweth, who was chatting with the math teacher and not watching Benji's lunch rebellion. Felix sighed and once again followed his partner.

"How much for a pretzel?" Benji asked.

"Two dollars." The pretzel man pointed to the sign.

"I'll give you one. It's all I got."

"Well, then you ain't got a pretzel." The man turned his back like he had another customer, which he didn't.

"I guess I'll starve."

Felix popped the last bite of sandwich into his mouth and was going to toss the plastic wrap when something caught his eye just a foot from the trash can—a red wallet with interlocking gold Cs. Two other kids walked right by it. For a second, he thought about leaving it and letting it be someone else's responsibility. But he picked it up. The leather was soft and smooth and somehow felt important.

He glanced around the park. No one appeared to be searching for it.

"What's that?" Benji came up behind him.

"Someone's wallet." Felix handed it to Benji. If he'd thought about it for even two seconds, he'd have realized this was a mistake.

Benji immediately unzipped it and pulled out a twenty-dollar bill.

"Score! Now we have lunch money."

Felix flinched. *I'm witnessing a robbery.*

Chapter $2

Benji Porter

Until this point, Felix had not been Benji's ideal field trip partner. He barely talked. He followed *every* rule. And he seemed to be against having any fun. But finding the wallet made up for all that, plus now they weren't going to starve.

Benji's stomach growled as if on cue.

"Put it back." Felix pointed at the twenty.

"We're just borrowing a few bucks. I'll return it." Benji dug around in the wallet. "I'll mail the money to . . ." He froze, staring at the driver's license in his hand.

"Whoa. Look." Benji held the ID an inch from Felix's face. "Laura Marie Friendly. Do you know who that is?"

Felix squinted at the driver's license.

"She's a freaking billionaire!" Benji shouted. Laura Friendly was the founder of Friendly Connect, a social media company that parents and grandparents loved.

"This lady is so loaded, she's building her own rocket ship to Mars. And once, she challenged a family to communicate using only Friendly Messenger for a week, and then paid them a million dollars."

"That can't be true," Felix said.

"Whatever. It's our lucky day. Pretzels on me. No, *hot dogs* on me." Benji smiled and shoved the wallet into the pocket of his sweatshirt. "Actually, on Laura Friendly."

He walked back to the cart. The pretzel man—who was also a hot dog man—glared at him until Benji held up the twenty.

"Two hot dogs, two sodas, and two bags of chips," Benji ordered.

"Anything else?" the hot dog–pretzel man asked.

"Stop. We shouldn't. It's stealing." Felix came up behind Benji. The kid made a great tail—like, FBI-level surveillance great.

The man folded his arms and raised his eyebrows.

"It's borrowing. Not stealing," Benji said through gritted teeth. "I'll pay it back. And I'm starving. A boy's gotta eat."

"Well?" the guy asked, growing impatient.

Benji sighed. "Make it one hot dog, one bag of chips, and one soda."

The man began filling the order while Felix stared at the ground like there were secret codes written on the sidewalk.

"I know you want a hot dog," Benji whispered.

Felix gave him the slightest nod, and Benji clapped him on the back.

"We're changing our order again. Two of each, and throw in some ice cream bars."

The price came to eighteen dollars, and Benji handed over the bill and said (for the first time in his life), "Keep the change."

They found a spot on the grass for their picnic. Close enough to the rest of the class not to be considered missing, but far enough away that Ms. Chenoweth couldn't see their upgraded lunch. Felix didn't talk as they ate. He scarfed down his food like he was hiding evidence.

"I bet Laura Friendly gives us a huge reward," Benji said as he opened his ice cream bar. "Like a million bucks."

"We need to pay her back and return the wallet." Felix chewed on his thumbnail. He was a skinny kid with red hair, freckles, and a big forehead. He always looked kind of nervous, but he appeared even shakier than usual.

"She doesn't need our money." Benji leaned back on the grassy hill. "I'm going to take the wallet home. Have my parents call her, maybe invite her—"

"No! We need to hand it in now." Felix's face was turning the color of the wallet.

"We *will* give it back, but we have to do it the right way to make sure we get a reward."

Felix jumped to his feet, and for the first time, Benji was forced to be the tail. They dumped their trash, even though

Benji still had a few bites of ice cream left. Felix practically ran to their teacher.

"Ms. Chenoweth, we found a wallet. It belongs to Laura Friendly."

Benji groaned. No use denying it. Of the two of them, everyone would call Felix the smart and trustworthy one. If it was Benji's word against Felix's, Benji wouldn't stand a chance.

"Excuse me?" Ms. Chenoweth said.

"Yep." Benji took out the red wallet. "Her address is in here. Felix and I can take an Uber or a taxi to her place. We'll be back in an hour. You won't even miss us."

"Hand it over," Ms. Chenoweth said, not even considering Benji's suggestion. As she looked through the wallet, her mouth dropped open.

"Let's give it to him." Felix motioned to a police officer waving kids off the sidewalk and into the park.

Ms. Chenoweth agreed it was the best option—though Benji still thought his taxi idea was better. She escorted the boys to the cop, who wasn't interested in the wallet until the mention of Laura Friendly's name.

"I'll make sure this gets returned," he said.

"You need to tell her *we* found it. Benji Porter and Felix Rannells. Partners." Benji threw an arm around Felix's shoulder, pulling him closer.

"Sure thing."

"He's not going to remember. He's not going to tell her," Benji complained to Ms. Chenoweth.

"Oh, here." Ms. Chenoweth sighed. She jotted a message on a piece of paper and slipped it into the wallet.

Found by Felix Rannells and Benji Porter. Students in Julie Chenoweth's class at Stirling Middle School in Stirling, NY.

"You promise not to take that paper out?" Benji asked.

"Yeah, kid."

Benji had no choice but to believe him. And to dream about the inevitable reward.

Chapter $3

Felix

Felix wasn't worried about the paper with their names coming out of the wallet; he was worried about getting the twenty dollars back in.

On the return bus ride to Stirling, Benji talked nonstop about how he'd spend his reward money. All Felix could think about was the bad luck that always accompanied bad decisions. In third grade, he'd lied about finishing his take-home reading, and the next day his mom had landed in the hospital with appendicitis. Logically, he knew the two events weren't related, but worrying didn't require logic.

"Maybe I'll buy the real Batmobile," Benji said.

"Can you just stop!" Felix finally snapped. "We shouldn't have taken the money. We stole."

"Geez. Calm down." Benji held up his hands.

"We broke the law."

"There's a difference between breaking a rule and bending a rule. We *borrowed* twenty bucks from a billionaire. We bent a law. Plus, we returned the wallet."

Felix gave up and turned to stare out the window. Benji would never see what they'd done as wrong.

When they arrived at the school, they exited the bus and didn't bother to say goodbye to each other.

"How was the field trip?" Felix's sister, Georgie, asked as he got into her truck.

"Fine. Where's Mom?"

"She took an extra shift at the nursing home." Georgie's red-brown hair was pulled up into a ponytail, and she wore sweatpants and a baggy Yankees sweatshirt that probably belonged to her fiancée, Michelle.

"Can we stop at McDonald's?" he asked.

"Do you have money? Because I don't." Georgie had a job but didn't make much as an assistant manager at Downtown Donuts.

"No," Felix mumbled. He thought again about the wallet and the twenty and Laura Friendly. She had money for McDonald's. That must be the life, being able to get fast food whenever you wanted, not just as a treat on your mom's payday.

"Sorry. I wish I could take you out," Georgie said. "Just make something when you get home. Okay?" She turned to him quickly and gave a sad smile. He hadn't meant to make her feel guilty.

Ten minutes later, they pulled up in front of the apartment complex. The buildings were royal blue with white trim, and each apartment had a small balcony. For almost a year, Felix and his mom had lived in a one-bedroom unit on the top floor. It was the nicest place they'd ever had.

"Do you need me to walk you in?" Georgie asked, faking a huge yawn.

"No. I'm fine," Felix lied. "Thanks for the ride." He got out and headed to building four.

Felix wasn't afraid to be home alone. He was twelve and capable of taking care of himself. But entering a dark and empty apartment made his heart race. He ran up the stairs two at a time even though his short legs weren't meant for the stretch, and then pulled out his key and opened the door.

A single light was on over the kitchen sink. The rest of the place was blanketed in darkness. Felix went from room to room—there weren't many—turning on lights and checking under the bed, in closets, and in the bathtub for a murderer. Rationally, he didn't expect to *actually* find a murderer or kidnapper behind the shower curtain. But he felt better knowing for sure.

No murderers. He was alone. Like always.

His mom had left him a note on the kitchen table.

Felix,
 I'll be home by midnight. Make yourself a
can of soup and do your laundry.
 Love,
 Mom

Doing laundry required money, and that gave Felix an idea. He grabbed the change jar from the counter and dumped it. He counted $8.25. That was all they had. He couldn't even pay back Laura Friendly for his half if he wanted to. And he definitely wanted to.

Chapter $4

Benji

Benji was standing in his bedroom, wearing only his underwear, when his mom barged in. He had the entire second floor to himself (three bedrooms, two bathrooms, only child), but still, Benji sometimes felt like he was suffocating.

"Mom!" He snatched a blanket off his bed and wrapped it around his waist.

"Sorry." She covered her eyes. "I didn't see anything. May I come in?"

"*May* I have a lock on my door?"

"No," she answered. It was an old argument. His dad had taken the lock off when Benji was five because he'd barricaded himself in and painted the walls with organic blueberry preserves. And in the seven years since, it seemed Benji hadn't earned back their trust.

"I reviewed your social studies essay." His ▮
out a paper bleeding in red ink.

"Thanks." He grabbed it. She insisted on ch▮
his homework and projects even though he also got extra
help at school for reading and writing.

"I think you're rushing through your work," she said.
"You need to take more time."

"That's not it. Even if I spent ten hours on it, it wouldn't
be any better. Words and me don't mix." In truth, he *had*
rushed the essay. But it was also true that more time
wouldn't make a difference.

"That's why I'm helping." His mom nodded. "Fix it before bed. It's due tomorrow, and you have a science test on
Friday." She knew better than he did about his due dates.

"Okay."

When he didn't say anything else, she left, and Benji
decided his homework and shower could wait. There was
something more important he had to do—his journal entry.
He didn't *actually* write in a diary. His entries were voice-
recorded on his iPad.

Benji had been forced to start journaling in fifth grade
after a recommendation at a parent-teacher conference.
*Benji may benefit from daily self-reflection using his own
words,* the teacher had noted. He didn't enjoy it at first, but
the journal became a useful tool. A couple of times a week,
he recapped the triumphs and struggles of his life. But the

Benji Porter recorded on the iPad wasn't real—not 100 percent real, anyway. It was a highly edited version of Benji Porter. A version that he hoped would make his parents happy.

And while the journal was intended to be private, Benji knew his parents listened to it. His entries were uploaded to the cloud, which they could access—and did.

But they didn't know he knew.

The secret to his success was finding the right balance. He couldn't come across as perfect. They *did* know him, after all. He just had to appear to be a hardworking, motivated, and overall good son.

October 26

Today I went on a field trip to New York to the natural history museum. The teacher made me be partners with a boy named Felix. He's shy and doesn't have any friends. I was picked so he wouldn't be lonely in New York. We saw about a hundred dinosaurs and watched an IMAX movie about Earth. At lunchtime, we went to Central Park. Felix found a wallet. It belonged to Laura Friendly. I convinced him to hand it over to the police.

Benji had told his parents about the wallet already. But he hadn't mentioned the *missing* twenty bucks then, and he wasn't going to mention it now.

> After dinner, Dad and I played basketball.
> I need to be ready for tryouts in a few weeks. I
> really want to make the seventh-grade team.

This was true. Benji *did* want to make the team. He needed to. Basketball was part of the Porter DNA. His dad had been a star player on his high school team, and Benji's mom had gone to Syracuse University on a basketball scholarship. Benji was the size of a basketball player (there was some DNA!), but he lacked any natural skills.

> That's about everything. I have a science test
> this week that I've been studying for a lot. Still, it's
> going to be super hard.
> Oh, and Mom walked in on me when I was prac-
> tically naked. I wish she'd knock.

> Over and out,
> Benji

Chapter $5

FRIDAY, OCTOBER 29

Felix

After school, Felix and about thirty other kids stood in a semicircle waiting for their names to be called for a team. Six captains had already been selected—a position based on popularity, not skills. This wasn't tryouts, which were still two weeks away. This was open gym, an opportunity just to play basketball.

Felix listened as the usual players were picked. Then it was Benji Porter's turn to select.

"I'll take my *buddy*, Felix."

Felix wasn't sure if he'd heard correctly. Benji, who was always a captain, had never chosen him. He usually selected other big kids.

"Interesting choice, Barney," Aidan Rozman, another captain, said. "We're going to destroy you."

Felix stepped forward, and Benji gave him a fist bump.

The game began, and Felix played point guard—a position that allowed him to control the tempo. Within two minutes, he realized that Aidan's team made mistakes when they played fast. So Felix pushed the ball up the court full-speed on every possession. He dribbled between his legs, passed behind his back, and moved side to side so quickly that the defender would slip. They didn't keep score during open gym, but Felix knew they were up by double digits when they took a water break.

As Felix drank from his bottle, Benji slapped him on the back.

"Good game, buddy. I should pick you more often."

"Thanks."

"You haven't found any wallets lately, have you? Or gotten any rewards?" Benji asked. Besides basketball, it was the only thing they had in common.

Felix shook his head. *Does he think I got a reward and I kept it for myself?*

"It's been three days," Benji continued. "How long does it take for someone to come up with a million-dollar prize?"

Felix had been thinking a lot about the wallet (and a possible reward). Like last night when his mom said she didn't have money for new sneakers as she dabbed superglue on his current pair where the rubber was pulling away at the bottom.

He also thought he might be cursed because of the

twenty. Bad things kept happening—more than usual. Like he'd accidentally left his library book on the bus. When he asked the driver this morning if anyone had handed it in, she said no. He checked every seat. It was gone. He didn't know how much it would cost to replace *Refugee*, but he knew he didn't have the money.

A whistle blew, and Felix took a last swig of water before running back to the court.

In the second half, Felix scored eight points, all on fast breaks, and had a couple of assists. He was having a great game until he got the ball just beyond the free-throw line, wide open.

"Shoot!" Benji yelled.

Felix hesitated, looking to drive to the basket.

"Shoot it!"

Felix knew it was a bad idea—his range was limited. But he bent his knees, pulled the ball to his shoulder, and shot. He used every muscle from his toes to his neck to heave the ball up.

He missed. Missed the rim. Missed the backboard. Missed everything.

"Air ball!" Aidan yelled, and soon his entire team was chanting.

"Lay off," Benji said to Aidan.

For the rest of the game, Felix didn't attempt another shot. *You don't miss shots you don't take.*

When the game was over, Felix pulled on his coat and put up the hood. As he left the gym, someone stepped on the back of his sneaker, making him trip and fly into the hallway. Instinctively, he threw out his arms to break his fall, and the fingers on his left hand bent backward.

"Ow!" He didn't mean to yell.

"You should be more careful." Aidan laughed and pushed his sweaty blond hair off his forehead. "Tryouts are coming up."

Felix rolled to his knees and kept his head down. He held his left hand to his chest.

"You okay?" Benji squatted next to him.

"Fine." Felix slowly bent his fingers, testing if they were broken. He could move them, but doing so was painful, and heat radiated from the joints between his hand and fingers.

"You need ice." Benji pulled Felix up by his right elbow.

"I said I'm fine." He was sure the fall was more bad luck, and he was sure it was because of the *stolen* twenty.

"Okay." Benji let go of Felix's arm.

"Did you give the money back to Laura Friendly?" Felix asked, knowing the answer.

"Nah. She doesn't need it."

Felix looked at Benji's new Jordans and thought Benji didn't need the twenty either.

"I'm serious. We need to pay her back. I'll pay my half. I just don't have any money right now. If you—"

"This is stressing you out," Benji interrupted, his head nodding as he spoke. "Come on. Follow me." They walked to the front of the building and to the line of cars waiting to pick up students. Benji pulled open the passenger-side door of a white SUV.

"Hey, Mom. Can I have twenty dollars?" Benji asked. "I owe Felix from the field trip." He motioned to Felix with his thumb.

"Hi, Felix. Nice to meet you." She reached into her bag without asking any questions and gave Benji a twenty-dollar bill.

"Thanks, Mom." Then Benji turned to Felix. "Here ya go."

Felix hesitated. It all seemed too easy, Benji's mom just pulling money from her wallet without a second thought. He tried to imagine a life where every dollar wasn't set aside for groceries or rent or emergencies.

"Better?" Benji asked.

"I'm going to send this to Laura Friendly."

"Good." Benji shrugged. "See ya." He climbed into the SUV, and it pulled away.

Felix didn't know where to send the money and wished he'd paid more attention to the address on Laura Friendly's license. Was it on the internet? Could you send cash in the mail? He'd figure it out. Things were going to get better.

But then Georgie joined him on the sidewalk, still dressed in her uniform from Downtown Donuts.

"The truck died. Again," she said. "Michelle is at work, and so is Mom. We're stuck here for at least an hour."

More bad luck. The twenty needed to be returned ASAP.

Chapter $6

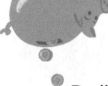

Benji

Benji stepped into social studies, and Mr. Platt sent him right back out.

"You're needed in the office." This was not an unusual request. Benji had spent his share of time across the desk from the principal—mostly for interrupting. Sometimes a dull class just required an impromptu sing-along.

When Benji walked through Mr. Palomino's office door, he spotted his smiling parents first. Then he saw Felix. Then Laura Friendly!

Reward time!

Laura Friendly looked different from the pictures on the internet—older and tired. She had white-blond hair, a pointy nose, and an unhappy expression. She sat rigid in the principal's chair, and a younger woman hovered behind her.

"Looks like we're all here," Mr. Palomino said. "Ms. Friendly, would you like to begin?"

"No." Everyone waited quietly for her to say more. Finally, she gestured toward the other woman. "Tracey."

"Laura is very thankful that you returned her wallet. She is impressed by your kindness and civility." Tracey focused on Felix and then Benji. "As a way of showing her gratitude, she is giving each of you a twenty-thousand-dollar college scholarship."

The short woman in maroon scrubs standing next to Felix shrieked and bounced around like a game show contestant. Then she hugged Felix, who was doing a perfect imitation of a garden gnome.

"Friendly Connect is also donating ten thousand dollars' worth of new technology to the school," Tracey continued.

"That's very generous." Mr. Palomino shook Laura Friendly's hand. The adults all started talking and saying thanks and how wonderful it all was.

A knock sounded on the door, and Ms. Hamilton, the front-desk lady, popped her head in.

"News Thirteen and the *Journal* are here. We're ready for the assembly."

"Thank you," Mr. Palomino said. "I guess it's showtime."

"What assembly?" Felix asked.

"Laura will make a short speech," Tracey answered.

"Then she will hand you each your scholarship check. We had large cardboard checks made. We thought they'd be fun keepsakes."

Laura Friendly closed her eyes and groaned. None of this seemed to be her idea. For someone who'd spent twenty million funding time-travel research (Benji saw it in a YouTube video), this was probably a boring use of her money.

"I'd like to talk to the boys alone," she said.

"Laura, we're on a schedule." Tracey's smile finally disappeared.

"I'll be quick."

The other adults filed out of the room. As soon as the door closed, Laura Friendly stood up.

"You found my wallet in the park?"

"Yes, ma'am," Benji said, and Felix nodded.

"And you turned it in to the authorities?" she asked.

"Yes, ma'am," Benji said again.

"But before honorably handing over my property, you stole twenty dollars."

Felix gasped like someone had hit him in the gut.

"No." Benji's voice cracked.

"I carry an emergency twenty dollars in my wallet," she said. "My father gave me a twenty when I left for college and told me to never be without my own cash."

"Was it the same twenty?" Felix asked, and Benji felt guilty for the first time.

"No, that was thirty years ago." Her eyebrows squished into a V.

"We took the money," Felix said rapidly. "We were hungry. We bought hot dogs. I'm sorry."

"You stole from me," she said.

"No, we borrowed from you," Benji said. "And we paid it back."

She crossed her arms. "Is that so?"

"Benji gave me the money to repay you." Felix pulled a folded bill from his pocket. "I didn't know where to send it."

"See, we're paying you back." Benji grabbed the twenty from Felix and tried to hand it to Laura Friendly, who refused to look at the money. "You don't even want it. Because you don't need it. Twenty bucks is like a penny to you. I wouldn't care if some kids took a penny from me to buy lunch."

"A penny still has value," she said.

Benji shrugged. "Technically."

"If I gave you a penny and it magically doubled the next day, and those pennies doubled the next day, and so on, do you know how much you'd have in a month?" Laura Friendly asked.

"You mean, like in thirty days? Or a short month like February?"

She pulled off her glasses and glared at Benji. "Yes, thirty days."

"I know it's a lot, but I need a calculator." He pulled his phone out of his pocket.

$0.01

$0.02

$0.04

$0.08

$0.16

$0.32

$0.64

$1.28

$2.56

$5.12

$10.24

$20.48

$40.96

$81.92

$163.84

$327.68

$655.36

$1,310.72

$2,621.44

$5,242.88

$10,485.76

$20,971.52

$41,943.04

$83,886.08

$167,772.16

$335,544.32

$671,088.64

$1,342,177.28

$2,684,354.56

$5,368,709.12

He gave her the answer.

"A penny isn't *nothing*. It can be the start of something big," she said.

"We get it." Benji had to concentrate on not rolling his eyes. "Aren't you supposed to ask us if we would rather have a million dollars now or a penny doubled every day for a month? That's the riddle math teachers like to give."

Laura Friendly tapped a finger on her chin. "What an interesting idea."

Benji had not expected her to say *that*.

"What if I offered you the scholarship money or a penny doubled every day for thirty days?"

"We'll take the penny doubled!" Benji grabbed Felix's arm and shook it. He couldn't believe this was happening.

"But . . ." Laura Friendly held up her hand. "You have to spend the penny-doubled money—the five million plus—in that same amount of time."

"Huh?" Benji didn't understand.

Someone knocked on the door.

"One more minute, please!" Laura Friendly snapped, and the door remained closed.

Felix swayed on his feet. Benji gestured for him to sit down before he fell over. But Felix shook his head.

"When I was a child, I stole a Crunch bar from a gas station," Laura Friendly began, taking a seat on the corner of the desk. "I must have been in fourth or fifth grade. I went inside to use the bathroom while my mother was pumping gas, and on my way out, I swiped the chocolate. I didn't eat it right away. I waited until we drove off. Of course, my mother knew I stole it, and she turned that car around, tires squealing. I was terrified. I thought she might drive me straight to the police station."

"Did she?" Benji asked.

"Of course not. We went back to the gas station. My mother paid for the Crunch and didn't even make me apologize. Then she bought the rest of the bars in the box. There were seventeen. When we got back in the car, she told me to eat them. All of them."

Laura Friendly shuddered and laughed.

"At first, it didn't seem like punishment at all. I ate three with no problems. Then my stomach hurt, and I was thirsty—very, very thirsty. My mother told me to keep eating, and you did *not* argue with my mother."

"Did you throw up all over her car?" Benji was sure he could down ten, but seventeen seemed vomit-inducing.

"Not *all* over the car." She leaned forward and stared at Benji. "I didn't eat chocolate again for twenty years."

He wondered if she had a point.

"Here's what's going to happen now. You can take the scholarship money, and we're done. Goodbye. Or you can take the five million plus and consume it all in thirty days." She paused and tapped her finger on her chin again. "And if you can do that, I'll give you a *real* prize: ten million *each* with no strings attached." She smiled for the first time— a creepy-clown grin that made Benji shiver.

"*Consume?*" Benji asked. "You mean we have to eat the money?"

"No. You need to spend it. All of it. But we'll need rules. Like no accumulation of assets."

"What does that mean?" Benji looked to Felix for an explanation, but the kid didn't seem capable of talking. *Can someone pass out and still remain standing?*

"It's like you've never taken an economics class." Laura Friendly rubbed the back of her neck. "Let me make it simple. No houses, no yachts, no planes. No stocks or bonds. No jewelry or art."

"Okay." Benji had never purchased jewelry or art in his life.

There was another knock. This time, the door opened, and Tracey stepped in.

"Laura, we have to do this now. Your plane is scheduled to leave at—"

"What's the point of having a private jet if I can't adjust the schedule?" Laura Friendly said. "Two more minutes. That's all we need. Right, gentlemen?"

"Fine." Tracey closed the door.

"So, what's it going to be?" Laura Friendly asked.

"We'll do it!" Benji said. "We'll take the bet."

Felix shook his head, and Benji was ready to strangle him. "I need to talk to my mom first."

"No. You can't tell anyone about the conditions of this challenge. You have to succeed on your own."

"Not tell anyone? You sound kinda creepy," Benji said.

"Maybe you're right." She crossed her arms. "Maybe this is a bad idea. Maybe we shouldn't—"

"No!" Benji couldn't tell if she was bluffing, but he wasn't willing to take a chance. "It's a good idea. A great idea. You're not creepy. You're brilliant."

"So, you accept my challenge?" Laura Friendly stood up and put her glasses back on.

"We'll do it!" Benji yelled. "This is going to be awesome."

"I need to hear it from both of you." Laura Friendly stared at Felix while Felix stared at his feet.

Come on, buddy!

Felix finally looked up. "Why are you doing this?"

She shrugged and then smiled again. "Because I can, and it's going to be tremendously fun to watch."

Chapter $7

Felix

Felix couldn't remember saying yes to Laura Friendly's offer, but he must have because he could remember Benji bear-hugging him hard enough to crack his back, and Ms. Friendly laughing like a cartoon villain, which made Felix sure they were walking right into her evil trap.

The rest of the afternoon was a blur. Laura Friendly announced her generous $5,368,709.12 "gift" in front of all the students at Stirling Middle. They screamed in excitement, and the adults sat stunned. Benji did a dance on the stage that would probably become a GIF, and he also spoke to a few reporters. Felix didn't speak or dance; he focused all his energy on just breathing.

Now Felix and his mom were sitting in a booth at Red Lobster, where it was easier to breathe, even though the whole place smelled like fish. She'd wanted to go out and celebrate his new fortune.

A waitress brought over a Coke for Felix and a tall multi-colored drink with three pieces of fruit around the rim for his mom. She didn't usually order fancy cocktails. And they didn't often go out to eat, especially somewhere nice like Red Lobster. The last time he was here was two years ago, when Georgie graduated from high school.

"Cheers." His mom raised her glass. "To my upstanding citizen and to your jackpot. You're a good kid, Felix. You deserve this."

He touched his glass to hers and forced a smile.

"Is everything okay?"

"It's a shock. That's all." Felix picked up his menu and studied it like there'd be a test on it later.

"This money is coming at a good time," she said. "Our lease is up in December. I'd planned to renew, but maybe we could consider a house." She smiled and shrugged. They'd never lived in a house before. "We'd have to look into it, but we could probably get the deed in your name. It would be like an investment."

He cringed at the word *investment*.

"Maybe," he said. "I don't know how this all works. I mean . . . I don't have *any* money yet. I can't even buy this dinner." Laura Friendly had announced the gift, but she hadn't written them a check. She'd told them it would take some time to get everything in order.

"You're right. We're getting ahead of ourselves." His

mom closed her menu. "Your poppy had a rule about money that I think we could adopt. He said, 'Never spend over one hundred dollars without sleeping on it first.' Good advice, huh?"

"Guess that means we shouldn't buy a house today." He'd never met his poppy, but he appreciated this insight from beyond the grave.

His mom laughed. "We will definitely have to sleep on it."

The waitress returned, and his mom ordered a trio of lobster dishes. Felix got the fried shrimp even though he didn't have an appetite.

"No work tonight?" Felix asked. His mother had two jobs: as a nurse's aide at an old folks' home (he wasn't supposed to call it *that*) and as a package sorter at an Express Services warehouse. She liked taking care of people, but handling boxes paid more.

"I took the rest of the day off. It's a special occasion when your son becomes a millionaire." She grabbed a cheddar biscuit and put it on a small plate.

She hadn't taken the day off on his birthday last month. *Guess that wasn't a special occasion.* But she had made him chocolate-chip waffles and bacon and had left them warming in the oven.

"I know it's your money, Felix." His mom couldn't stop talking about the millions. "But I think it would be nice if we could help out Georgie and Michelle, too. Maybe with a small loan."

"Yeah." His sister and her fiancée both had jobs, and he knew they were trying to save for a wedding and a house and a new truck.

Felix felt like the world's strongest rubber band was squeezing his head. He needed to tell his mom the truth.

He wasn't a *real* millionaire. At least not yet.

But if he did win, and he did get ten million free and clear, he would buy his mom a house. And one for Georgie and Michelle, too.

If!

Tuesday, November 2

Felix was sitting at the kitchen table, eating off-brand frosted flakes and focusing on the maze on the back of the box, when the TV caught his attention.

"Tech billionaire Laura Friendly surprised two students at a middle school in Stirling, New York, yesterday," the woman behind the news desk said.

"Mom! Come here!" he called. She was still in her bedroom, getting ready for work.

The image on the screen cut away from the reporter and to the assembly at school.

"The boys found Friendly's wallet last week in Central

Park and turned it in to the NYPD. As a reward for their efforts, she gave the students—you're not going to believe this—$5,368,709.12." A graphic popped up on the TV along with a cha-ching sound effect.

His mom walked into the living room with her hair still wet from a shower. Felix pointed to the TV, and her mouth dropped open.

Benji was on the screen. "We just returned the wallet because it was the right thing to do. We never expected anything like this." Felix-from-yesterday was in the background of the video. He looked ghostly white, and his eyes darted around the room like something was about to attack him.

"There you are!" His mom pointed.

"I look like a freak."

"No, you're handsome," his mom said, because that was what moms were supposed to say.

The news anchors came back on, showing off their best surprised faces—mouths open and eyes wide, like the emoji.

"This is national!" his mom shrieked. "People across the country will see this."

Do you think Mark is watching? He couldn't ask the question out loud. His father was not part of their lives, and hadn't been for years.

"That's quite a reward for a returned wallet," one host said. "When I left my bag in a cab, I only gave the driver a twenty when he returned it. That was a few years ago. Now the going rate seems to be over five million dollars."

Both hosts laughed.

Felix's mom muted the TV. "You're a celebrity. I bet you think people will clean up after you now." She winked at him and snatched a blanket off his bed, which was also their couch. The apartment had only one bedroom, and he slept on the pullout in the living room. His mother called it cozy and easy to clean. He couldn't argue with that.

"Sorry, I'll do it." Felix got up and began folding the blankets and sheets.

As he transformed his bed back into a couch, his mom's cell chimed. It was the only phone they had between the two of them. She answered and then glanced in his direction, smiling.

"Thank you," she said multiple times before hanging up. Then she pointed to Felix. "No school today. We're going to the bank to get your money."

Chapter $8

Benji

Someone from Laura Friendly's office called early that morning and instructed the Porters to meet at First Bank of New York at ten o'clock.

Things keep getting better, Benji thought. *Five million bucks and no school.*

When they arrived, Benji and his parents were escorted to a room with a large wooden table surrounded by leather chairs. Two of the seats were already occupied by guys in suits, who stood as the Porter family entered.

Benji had hoped to see piles of cash on the table. The largest bill the US Mint made was a hundred-dollar bill—he'd Googled it last night. That would be over fifty thousand bills. If they were all put into one stack, it would be about seventeen feet high. Or they could make seventeen one-foot-tall stacks. (He'd spent a lot of time Googling money.)

Felix and Ms. Rannells walked in a few minutes later. Felix took a seat without saying anything and immediately stared at his hands in his lap.

"Good morning, I'm Roger McDowell, Laura Friendly's personal attorney." Then he motioned to the other man. "And this is Leonard Trulz, an accountant for this endeavor. We have a lot of paperwork to get through, so let's begin. The money's been placed in an account here at the bank in the names of Felix Heathcliff Rannells, Benji Augustine Porter, and Laura Marie Friendly."

"Ew, we both have horrible middle names," Benji said.

Felix didn't even pretend to laugh at the comment.

"Excuse me. Why is she on the account?" Benji's dad asked.

"It's necessary so we can address the tax burden," the lawyer explained. "It's a custodial account."

"Will we have access to the funds too?" Ms. Rannells asked.

"No. Only the boys can write electronic checks and use the associated debit cards."

"That's ridiculous. They're twelve," Benji's mom said.

"Maybe we should have *our* lawyer present." Benji's father shook his head and then pulled out his cell phone.

"I'm sorry if I gave you the wrong impression." Mr. McDowell clasped his hands and folded them on top of a stack of documents. "This is not a negotiation. It's a take-it-or-leave-it offer."

Benji watched the muscle in his father's jaw tighten. He was a pretty even-tempered guy, but that slight movement was a clue—he was royally ticked off.

His dad put down the cell phone. "Continue, please."

Papers flew around the table, requiring signatures. Then the boys were issued debit cards—thick black cards with their names printed in silver letters.

"I assume each of the boys is entitled to half the money. How will that be monitored?" Benji's mom asked.

"There is no formal arrangement for dividing the money," Mr. McDowell answered.

"Can we set up two separate accounts?" his mom asked.

"No," Mr. McDowell replied.

"Are you kidding me? This is wrong," Benji's dad said. When they'd left for the bank, Benji's dad had been all smiles. Now he looked like he'd been robbed and kicked between the legs.

"Remember, take it or leave it." Mr. McDowell sat back in his chair and crossed his arms.

Benji's parents didn't get it. They were not in charge, and they had to let him do this, or they could say goodbye to the money.

"Proceed," Benji's dad replied.

McDowell pushed another set of papers to the parents. Benji's dad didn't even bother to read it before he signed.

"Thank you very much, Ms. Rannells and Mr. and Mrs. Porter." The lawyer collected the papers and put them in a folder. "Now we need to speak to Felix and Benji alone for a moment. Laura Friendly has prepared a statement that I must read to them. Once that is taken care of, we're done, and your sons will be millionaires."

Those words did the trick. Smiles returned, and the parents left the room without argument.

Mr. McDowell let out a noisy breath before zeroing his dark eyes on Benji and then Felix. "Boys, you understand you aren't simply receiving this money without stipulations. Correct?"

"Yeah," Benji answered. "It's a game."

"A very expensive game," Mr. McDowell replied, and it was obvious that he did not approve. He'd probably feel different if he'd been the one invited to play.

Mr. McDowell slid a packet of papers in front of each boy. Benji picked it up to read, but he couldn't get past the first few lines. He *could* read. But his brain got distracted like four different songs were playing at once and he was expected to sing along to only one.

Thankfully, Mr. McDowell went over the document.

"The opening paragraph simply states that you have until midnight on December first to spend $5,368,709.12. At that time, if the account balance is zero, you will each receive ten million with no restrictions. Are we clear so far?"

"Yep," Benji said.

Felix nodded.

"Section two outlines additional rules. Number one says you cannot simply give the money away. Not to people. Not to charities." The lawyer cleared his throat. "Number two states you cannot buy gifts for others."

"Like birthday presents?" Benji asked.

"Like *any* presents." Leonard Trulz finally spoke. He hardly had any hair on the top of his white head but had very bushy eyebrows and a mustache—like three fat gray caterpillars. "You cannot buy *things* for other people. Not a TV. Not a bouquet of flowers. Not a pair of socks. However, you can take someone out to eat, throw parties, and go to events. If you are sharing the experience, it is permissible."

"That leads us to rule three," Mr. McDowell said. "You must use what you purchase. For example, if you purchase a plane ticket, you must take the trip. If you buy a new suit, you must wear that suit. If you buy a computer, you must use the computer."

"Got it." Benji drew an invisible check mark in the air with his finger.

Mr. McDowell turned a page of the document. "The fourth rule in section two is the 'No List.' Things you cannot buy."

Benji only half listened to the no list. All these rules were only temporary.

"Lastly, you may not tell anyone about the challenge,

including parents. No one is to know this is a *game*—as you put it."

"*No* problem." This would be the biggest secret Benji had ever kept.

"And finally, section three," the lawyer continued. "At the end of thirty days, everything purchased with this money will be repossessed."

"What? Why?" Benji asked.

"It's to prohibit you from making a profit. You cannot have a giant garage sale when it's over."

That would have been a good idea.

Mr. McDowell spun the paper around. "That's it. Signatures, please."

Benji scribbled his name on the line. Felix just stared at the papers as he chewed on his thumbnail.

"Come on, buddy," Benji said. "We got nothing to lose. Even if we don't finish the game, we're still going to have the best month of our lives."

Felix placed his hands on the table. Benji wished he would say something. Benji wasn't used to being around someone so quiet. His friends talked nonstop.

"We can do this," Benji whispered.

Felix took a breath, grabbed a pen, and signed his name. Benji watched to make sure Felix didn't write *no way* or something like that.

"Thank you." Mr. McDowell collected the papers. "Mr. Trulz, why don't you explain your role."

"Certainly." Mr. Trulz sat up straighter. "We will be communicating extensively over the next thirty days. My job is to monitor and approve *all* spending."

"I get it. You're our accountant," Benji said.

"Essentially. Any swipe of your debit card or electronic payment, I will be notified immediately. I'm here to enforce the agreement and to interpret the rules. If you have questions, I'm merely a phone call away. Day or night. Of course, I want you to succeed, but I will insist you play fairly." Mr. Trulz crossed his arms and gave them an I-dare-you-to-challenge-me look.

"That's it. Meeting adjourned." The lawyer stood up and offered his hand to Benji and then Felix. "Good luck, boys. Enjoy the *game*."

Rules of Play

Section 1
Spend $5,368,709.12 by midnight on December 1.

Section 2
1. Cannot give away the money.
2. Cannot buy physical gifts for people.
3. Must use what is purchased.
4. No List:

    Real estate

    Vehicles

    Jewelry

    Art

    Investments (stocks, bonds, etc.)

    Companies

    Trademarks or copyrights

    Anything illegal

    Items on eBay

5. Cannot tell anyone about this challenge and these rules.

Section 3
On December 2, any items purchased with the $5,368,709.12 will be repossessed.

Chapter $9

TUESDAY, NOVEMBER 2

Felix

Only the boys remained in the bank conference room, and Felix sat frozen in his chair. It was quarter past eleven. If today had been a normal day (would he ever have a normal day again?), he'd have been in math class.

Benji was anything but frozen. He galloped around the table like he was riding an invisible bronco, waving his plastic debit card over his head and making whooping sounds.

"We're millionaires, Felix!"

"Not really," Felix mumbled, and picked up his debit card for the first time. It had a weight to it that couldn't be measured in ounces.

"What are you talking about?" Benji hopped on the corner of the table and held out his cell phone for Felix. The banking app, which Mr. Trulz had set up, was open, and the account balance showed $5,368,709.12. "According to this, we're millionaires. According to everyone, we're millionaires."

"It's temporary."

Benji made a sputtering sound. "Everything is temporary. Even the sun. It'll burn out eventually, like in a million years."

It's closer to five billion years.

Benji drummed his fingers on the table and stared at Felix. "So, what do you want to do first?"

Felix shrugged. "Make a plan."

"You sound like my mom. Have you been talking to my mom?" Benji gave him an accusing glare. "Listen, Felix. You can make a to-do list tomorrow. Now let's have some fun. We have millions and a free afternoon. What do you want to do, buddy?"

Felix knew Benji was looking for a big idea, like swimming with great white sharks or running bases at Yankee Stadium. *(Are those activities you can actually buy?)* But what Felix really wanted was to get something that every kid at Stirling already had.

"So, what's it going to be?" Benji wriggled his eyebrows.

"I want a cell phone."

"That's it?"

Felix nodded. "Yeah. For now. Until we have a plan."

"Okay. Have fun with that." Benji jumped off the table.

"I'm going to go see if I can take flying lessons and go sky-diving. Six Flags is closed for the season. How much do you think they'd charge to reopen it for the afternoon?"

Felix shrugged.

"Have fun phone-shopping." Benji pulled open the conference room door. "Let's meet tomorrow before school. Seven a.m. at the Market Street Diner. We'll work on your plan then."

"I don't know if I can get a ride." His mom's schedule changed from day to day.

"You're a millionaire, Felix. Figure it out."

Wednesday, November 3

And Felix did figure it out. Using his new iPhone, he'd texted Georgie and asked for a ride in the morning. In exchange, he'd taken her and Michelle to dinner. They'd chosen the place, and that was how Felix had ended up at Red Lobster for the second night in a row.

At 6:55 a.m., Felix was sitting alone in a booth near the front window of the Market Street Diner. A waitress brought over a menu and jokingly offered him coffee. He watched the parking lot as a red Volkswagen pulled up with Benji in the backseat. Both the driver and Benji got out, and they shook hands before heading inside. Benji joined Felix, and the driver sat alone.

"I'm starving." Benji grabbed the menu out of Felix's hands.

Felix was hungry too but was more interested in coming up with a plan than ordering food.

"Did you get a phone?" Benji asked.

"Yeah." Felix held up his new toy. "Benji. I think we're in trouble. I figured out how much we have to spend every day." Felix had wasted most of the evening playing with his phone and the rest of the time stressing over money.

"About a hundred and seventy thousand dollars," Benji said, not looking up from the menu. "I did my homework too, and I just opened the banking app. We only spent about ten thousand on day one."

"Ten thousand? How?" Felix had only used his debit card for the iPhone (and a one-month activation) and his Red Lobster dinner. "And I need that app."

Benji helped him set it up.

"I ordered a new computer and stuff online. And Aidan, Luke, and I went to laser tag, and an arcade, and a go-cart track. I would have invited you, but I didn't have your number."

The waitress returned. "Morning, boys. You do have money, right?"

"More than we know what to do with." Benji ordered blueberry pancakes, a western omelet, an egg-and-biscuit sandwich, and French toast.

Felix went with a waffle and a side order of bacon.

FIRST BANK OF NEW YORK

Current Balance: $5,359,556.04

RECENT TRANSACTIONS

Nov 2, Cheeseburger Heaven	-$118.80
Nov 2, ComputersAndGaming.com	-$1,860.32
Nov 2, Laser Tag Adventure	-$180.00
Nov 2, Red Lobster	-$171.72

"Seriously, I don't think it's possible, spending that much every day." Felix had done some simple calculations. Spending $178,956.97 meant they could buy 716 pairs of sneakers a day (if the sneakers cost $250 each). But the rules said the boys each had to use what they purchased. So if they each wore 358 pairs a day, and they were awake for sixteen hours a day, they'd have to change their shoes every 2.68 minutes. Every day! For a month!

"It's not going to be easy, but it'll be awesome." Benji smiled and shrugged. He didn't look worried at all. "First, I think we should quit school."

"What?"

"Just for the month. Spending money is a full-time job."

"That's dumb," Felix said.

"Don't call me dumb!" Benji's face hardened, and he looked ready to hit something. Maybe Felix.

"I didn't. Sorry. I meant the idea."

"Never mind." Benji smiled again, but it didn't look genuine. "We need to get a fancy place to live. And since we can't buy a mansion, we should rent a penthouse at the nicest place around, like the Grand Regency. It's only twenty minutes away. And it has a pool."

"I don't know if my mom will—"

"Stop right there." Benji held up a hand. "You aren't going to get through this without disappointing your mom. She might even get mad. Have your parents ever been mad at you?"

Felix shrugged. His mom rarely got upset with him, but he *rarely* did anything to get upset over. His father didn't care enough to get mad at him. Felix hadn't seen Mark in four or five years, and the last time had been by accident. They'd bumped into him at a gas station near Syracuse. It was a quick handshake and a "See ya soon."

Mark didn't care about Felix, but maybe he'd care about the money.

The waitress returned with platters of food. Most of it would be thrown away (though they'd be sure to take at least one bite of everything). As Felix finished his waffle, he glanced up at the TV, which had the current time and temperature in the corner.

"We have to go!" He jumped out of the booth. "How are we getting to school?" He hadn't considered that when Georgie had dropped him off.

"Uber. Relax, buddy." Benji calmly waved the waitress over.

She gave them the bill, and Benji immediately called Mr. Trulz. "Are we allowed to tip a thousand dollars to a nice waitress?" The answer was no. Their tipping was limited to 20 percent. Benji paid theirs and the Uber driver's tab. Then they crawled into the backseat of his car.

"Felix, meet Reggie." Benji took care of introductions.

Reggie put an arm awkwardly into the backseat as he drove, and Felix shook it.

"Nice to meet you." Reggie had black hair that he wore in a man bun, a short beard, and thick-rimmed glasses.

"I've hired Reggie to be our driver for the month," Benji said to Felix. "We have a lot of business to attend to, and we can't be waiting around for an Uber or a Lyft."

Felix had not spent a single minute waiting for an Uber or Lyft in his life.

"Benji made me an offer I couldn't refuse. I tried, but he wouldn't get out of my car until I accepted." Reggie laughed.

"We're paying him a thousand dollars a day from now

until December first, with a ten percent daily raise if he's a good employee."

Felix had no idea how much a chauffeur should make. A thousand per day seemed like a lot of money, but it was a mere blip of the total they had to spend.

"Did you run it by Mr. Trulz?" Felix asked.

"Yep," Benji said. "The *troll* approved it. Took care of everything. But Reggie is unavailable on Monday and Wednesday mornings between nine and noon."

"And some Tuesday evenings I've got study group," Reggie added. "I'm majoring in philosophy at the University at Albany. I have to think about my future."

"We're not going to stand in the way of the man's education," Benji added.

Suddenly, Reggie hit the brakes hard. The seat belt tightened across Felix's chest, and his head whipped forward.

"Dang, dog!" Reggie yelled.

Felix hadn't seen the dog run into the road, but he spotted him in a Waffle House parking lot now. A scrawny gray-brown thing with long matted fur.

Reggie slowly drove past.

"Stop the car," Felix said.

"I swear, I didn't hit him," Reggie said.

"Just stop, please."

Reggie pulled over in the parking lot, and Felix jumped

out. The dog either didn't notice or didn't care. He was too busy eating through a crumpled fast-food bag. As Felix approached, an awful stench filled the air. He didn't know if it was coming from the dog or the nearby dumpster.

"Here, boy," he whispered.

The dog glanced at Felix, but he wasn't about to give up his free meal.

Felix slowly walked to the mutt and patted his head. The dog's head came to Felix's midthigh, and his tail was short, like part of it was missing.

"What are you doing?" Benji yelled from the car.

Felix shrugged. He hadn't really thought about what he was doing. It just felt like fate. The wallet, Laura Friendly, the money, breakfast with Benji, hiring Reggie had all led to this moment.

The stray seemed to sense it too. He stopped nosing in the bag and leaned against Felix's leg.

"Felix, let's go. Remember, you're the one who doesn't want to quit school."

"Coming!" Felix decided that if the dog was truly meant to be his, he would follow Felix back to the car.

Felix walked.

The dog followed.

Chapter $10

WEDNESDAY, NOVEMBER 3

Benji

"What are you doing?" Benji asked Felix as the stray dog jumped into the backseat. The smell of garbage and slobber filled the car.

"Whoa!" Reggie said. "That dog stinks. Get it out."

"Sorry," Felix said. "I'll clean your car later. Please let him stay."

The mongrel jumped into Benji's lap, and Benji shoved him off. He imagined the fleas and ticks crawling from the dog onto him, and it made him itchy.

"What are you going to do with him?" Benji asked.

"I'm adopting him." Felix smiled wide. Benji had never seen Felix look happy.

"Buddy, you shouldn't be adopting a stray dog. You should buy a purebred—something expensive. We're millionaires. Don't forget."

"I want this dog." Felix didn't seem to mind having the filthy mutt crawling over him. He rubbed the matted ears and let the dog lick his cheek.

Benji fought the urge to vomit.

"It's fate," Felix said. "The money, the diner, Reggie. It all led to this *good boy*. The dog and I are meant to be. Fate."

"Felix." Reggie spun in his seat to face the boys. "You're describing determinism, not fate. *Determinism* means one event leads to another to another to another. All those events led to this dog. While *fate* means that regardless of what you did this morning—rode with me, took the bus, walked—you would have met this stinky mutt."

"Okay." Felix shrugged. "Then it was determinism. Determined to happen."

Reggie nodded slowly and then started driving again. "You should read Baron d'Holbach if you want to know more about hard determinism."

"What are you going to do with him while we're at school?" Benji asked.

Felix stared at the roof of the car before answering. "Reggie? Can I hire you to watch my dog? At least for today?"

"How much?" Reggie asked.

"How about a thousand dollars?" Felix shrugged and looked at Benji. "I'll call Mr. Trulz and set it up."

"And I'll throw in another thousand if you get the dog a bath," Benji added. He didn't think he could talk Felix out of adopting the mutt. At the very least, they needed a clean one.

"No problem," Reggie said. He pulled up in front of the school. "You're also paying to get my car detailed."

Felix nodded enthusiastically. "Whatever he needs, we'll pay for it."

"You going to name him?" Reggie asked.

Felix didn't answer right away. He rubbed the dog under the chin, and then a bigger smile spread across his face.

"His name is Freebie."

"Just perfect." Benji rolled his eyes.

Felix quietly professed his love to Freebie before saying goodbye and thanks to Reggie. Benji had never witnessed love at first sight until just then.

"You ready for this?" Benji asked as they reached the front door of the school.

"For what?"

"You're not the Felix you were two days ago," Benji warned him as they stepped inside.

Every head turned in their direction, and as they walked to the seventh-grade hallway, kids held up their hands, and Benji high-fived them. Felix shoved his hands into his pockets. Just like that, he'd gone back to his turtle-hiding-in-his-shell look.

"You going to be okay?" Benji asked when they reached Felix's locker.

"Yeah."

"If you're not okay, you can tell me." Benji grabbed Felix's shoulders and forced him to look at him. "I don't expect us to be best friends, but the only way this is going to work is if we're honest with each other. Completely honest." Benji felt a little twitch in his neck muscles, lecturing someone about honesty.

"Got it."

"If you need to talk to someone, come to me. Don't tell anyone about the challenge."

"I know." Felix pushed away Benji's hands.

"Good. I gotta take care of some stuff." Benji patted Felix on the back, and then he dashed into the boys' bathroom, intending to make some calls, but Aidan followed him in.

"Hey, Benji. Let's do something after school. Your treat." Aidan laughed. "What about paintball?"

"Can't today. I gotta meet up with Felix." Benji shrugged. "Maybe over the weekend."

"Whatever." Aidan crossed his arms. "Must be nice being a millionaire. Too bad you have to share with Felix."

"Not like I had a choice." Benji didn't *hate* Felix, but just about any other guy at Stirling would have been more fun.

"You should have told Laura Friendly that you and me found the wallet." Aidan sighed. "I'm sure you'll make it up to me, Barney."

The bell rang, and Aidan rushed off to homeroom. Benji

stayed to make his phone call. He found the number for Little Italy Pizza and Pasta and ordered two hundred pizzas to be delivered to the school at 11:00 a.m.

"Some cheese, some pepperoni, some meatball, some onion and pepper. Just no mushrooms. Got it?"

"Some people like mushrooms," the woman replied.

"I don't understand how people can eat fungus. But fine, one mushroom pizza. Just one." Benji pulled out his debit card. "And can you make this a standing order? I need pizzas every day—or every school day."

"As long as you've got the money, honey, I've got the pies. I can probably get you a discount—"

He cut her off. "No discount."

"Fine by me. That'll be $2,398 plus tax and tip."

"No problem."

"I gotta say, I don't know if this is a wise use of your money."

"Don't worry about that," Benji said. "Just keep 'em coming until December first."

•   •   •

Benji beamed as he looked around the cafeteria. His free pizza lunch was a success. Students smiled and laughed. Teachers chatted and didn't care about the noise level for a change. Every slice spread happiness and joy. Maybe his pizza initiative would wipe out bullying and homework at Stirling Middle School.

But then Alma Miranda walked past him and didn't stop for pizza. He'd always considered Alma unique—maybe even weird. Her mouth was constantly moving like she was singing to herself, but she didn't make any sound. She could touch her tongue to her nose. (Though he hadn't seen her do that since fifth grade.) And she wore the same thing every day—a black shirt, black jeans, and some kind of strange hair thingy. Today, a purple headband with a unicorn horn held back her dark curls. He imagined that her hair smelled as pretty as it looked.

"Hey, Alma. You want some pizza?" he asked, his voice cracking. "It's free."

"No, thank you. I brought my lunch." She held up a bag shaped like a cocker spaniel.

"But it's pizza." He gestured. No lunch from home could compete with pizza. No *food*—other than maybe desserts and, occasionally, a cheeseburger—could compete with pizza.

"Yes. It is." She gave him a look like she was talking to a four-year-old. He'd never noticed how brown and warm her eyes were before, like hot chocolate.

Alma took a seat at an empty table in the back of the cafeteria. Benji followed and plopped onto the bench across from her. Then, as if his body was new to his brain, he didn't know what to do with his arms or what to say.

"Have you ever tried pizza?" *What kind of question is that, Benji?*

"Of course." She laughed, and his face felt warm.

Then he noticed the NUT-FREE ZONE sticker on the corner of the table.

"Are you allergic? To dairy or crust?" he asked hopefully. "I'm going to order pizza every day, and tomorrow I can get you whatever you want."

"I'm not allergic. I just don't like to waste food." She opened her lunch bag and pulled out a green wrap filled with more green stuff. It looked like something his mom would eat.

"It's good pizza." Benji couldn't control the words coming out of his mouth.

Stop talking about pizza!

She snorted. "Why are you pushing the pizza so hard? Do you get another million dollars for every slice we eat?"

"No." He flinched at the suggestion. It wasn't exactly accurate, but there was some truth to it.

"You okay?" She squinted at him.

"Yeah. Enjoy your lunch." Benji got up from the table.

"You too," she said. Then she took out a book. It felt like every other kid in the cafeteria was eating the lunch Benji had bought. Some were eating two lunches—pizza and cafeteria food. But Benji could only focus on the one person who'd turned it down.

Chapter $11

WEDNESDAY, NOVEMBER 3

Felix

"Felix, you be a captain," Jeremy Hollands suggested.

"Okay." Felix stepped forward, and for the first time, he got to select *his* basketball team. But he couldn't pick Benji (not that he would anyway), because Benji was also a captain. And while there were six teams for the three courts, everyone wanted to see Team Felix and Team Benji go head-to-head.

Benji sank the first shot of the game. It was the only time his team led. Felix's guys scored on nearly every possession. Benji got a few more baskets and blocked half a dozen shots, but he fouled just as often.

"Good game," Felix said at the end, and offered Benji a high five.

"Was it?" Benji asked, not slapping Felix's hand. "Let's go. Reggie and your dog are waiting in the parking lot."

Felix grabbed his stuff and ran to the Volkswagen. He hadn't forgotten he had a dog, but he still couldn't believe it. He pulled open the back door and was greeted by a mutt that looked and smelled much different than he had in the morning.

Freebie's fur was short, and he even had a few bald spots. His big brown eyes were no longer covered with doggy bangs. He smelled of baby powder and wore a plaid bandanna and a leather collar.

"Whoa? You sure this is the same dog?" Benji asked as they crawled into the backseat.

"Freebie needed a flea dip, a bath, and a full buzz cut." Reggie reached into the backseat and gave the dog a treat, and handed Felix a receipt for $169.17.

Freebie's half tail whipped in excitement.

"Also took him to the vet. Your dog needed shots and medicine for worms. Wasn't cheap." Reggie handed them more papers. "And finally, you detailed my car. Nice, right?" A receipt for $471.26 from the vet and $99 from the car wash.

"Yeah," Benji said. "I'll call the troll. Get you paid."

"So where to, boss?" Reggie asked.

"I live at the Mayfield Apartments," Felix said. "It's near—"

"No," Benji interrupted. "I told you at breakfast. We need a nice place to stay for a while." He leaned forward. "Reggie, take us to the Grand Regency."

"You got it. Put on your seat belts." Reggie drove out of the school parking lot.

"If I'm not going home, I guess I should tell my mom." Felix pulled out his phone to text her. He didn't want to say he was checking out a fancy hotel, but that was the truth.

FELIX: I'm hanging out with Benji

FELIX: We're going to the Grand Regency

FELIX: Can you meet me there after work please

His phone buzzed a few seconds later. He braced himself for the reply.

MOM: Why are you going to a hotel?

MOM: What's going on?

Felix didn't answer. Instead, he opened the camera app and tried to get pictures of Freebie, which was impossible to do in a moving car with a moving dog.

"You played good today," Benji said. "What did you have? Forty points?"

Benji was exaggerating. Felix had only scored sixteen.

"Thanks. You did good too."

Benji grunted. "No, I didn't. I played better last week when we were on the same team."

"Yeah. Maybe."

"We're here," Reggie announced a few minutes later. "Do I need to open the door for you? I'm new to the chauffeur business."

"Don't worry. We got it," Benji said.

Reggie handed Felix a leather leash that matched Freebie's collar. "He's a runner. Keep him tight."

"Thanks." Felix attached the leash. Then he went to grab the door handle, but someone pulled it open from the outside.

"Good afternoon, welcome to the Grand Regency. Checking in?" a man in a dark suit with gold buttons asked.

Freebie barked like he'd never seen a doorman before, which could totally be true. Felix had only seen them on TV.

"Yeah, checking in," Benji answered, getting out on his side. "Reggie, come with us. We'll probably need an adult."

They walked through the lobby with its shiny white floor, giant chandelier, and fish-filled pond. Freebie pulled desperately toward the water. Felix didn't know if the dog wanted to go swimming or fishing.

Benji spoke to the woman behind a marble counter about rooms. She didn't take them seriously until she realized they were Laura Friendly's millionaire boys. After that, things were simple.

Benji booked the Presidential Suite for himself—though he offered it to Felix first. Felix got the smaller Capital Suite, which allowed dogs for a fee, and they rented Reggie a deluxe room because Benji figured they might need him at a moment's notice. They paid for all three in full through December first.

"Let's check out our new home," Benji said, taking his key.

A bellman retrieved their backpacks from the car and led them to Benji's Presidential Suite on the top floor. When he pushed open the double doors, Felix felt like they were entering a new world.

The living room had three leather couches, a TV bigger than a SMART Board, a glass bar with six stools, a grand piano, a fireplace in which a fire was already burning, and a life-sized marble horse statue. And the windows! There seemed to be no outside walls, just windows. The Albany skyline in one direction, the sun just setting, and rolling hills in the other.

The bellman explained some of the suite's features. There were buttons for everything—to lower the blinds, to change the lights from normal to blue, to call for a butler!

"This must be where the president or YouTube stars stay when they visit Albany." Benji jumped from one couch to another, then to the third.

Felix dropped Freebie's leash and let him run around the room. He too jumped from one couch to another.

"If you need anything, please don't hesitate to call," the bellman said as he left the room.

"Hey, take my picture," Benji said as he tried to climb onto the marble horse.

"Okay." Felix pulled out his phone, and he noticed five missed calls from his mom. He snapped a few pictures for Benji, then called her.

"Where are you?" she asked.

"At the Grand Re—"

She cut him off. "What room, Felix?"

"Our room is fourteen-oh-five."

"Our room? I'm coming up." She didn't say goodbye.

"I gotta go." Felix grabbed Freebie by his leash and took the elevator down one floor. He used his key card to open his door. His suite was half the size of Benji's presidential palace, and he only had a minute to look around, but he knew it was the nicest place he'd ever stayed.

His mom knocked—more like pounded—on the door. Freebie barked and lunged.

"Calm down." Felix held the leash tight as he pulled open the door.

His mom stood in the doorway in her maroon scrubs, her dyed hair pulled into a ponytail. She was short, but still a few inches taller than Felix.

"Whose dog is that?"

"Mine. This is Freebie." Felix pulled Freebie close and scratched him under the chin until the dog calmed down.

"Felix, what's going on?" His mom slid into the room, staying next to the wall to keep out of Freebie's reach. "Why do you have a dog?"

He shrugged. "I wanted a dog." It was a two-year-old's response but also the truth. A real pet had never been possible before.

"And I want a house on the beach in Hawaii. 'I want' is not an acceptable answer."

"Freebie needed a home."

She put her hands on her hips. "And why do you have a hotel room?"

"Um . . ."

The hotel had been Benji's idea, but looking around, Felix liked the place. The living room had a huge television. The balcony looked toward the city. There were two bedrooms, which meant two beds.

"I don't want to sleep on a couch anymore," he mumbled.

In an instant, his mom's face transformed from angry to sad. Felix felt guilty and wished she would go back to angry.

"I'm sorry, Mom. I should have asked first," he said. "But it's just temporary. We have a lot to figure out. And why not do it somewhere nice?"

His mom dropped into a leather chair. Freebie inched closer, smelling her shoes, and she reached down to pet his head.

"Temporary," she repeated.

"I promise." If she only knew how true that was.

FIRST BANK OF NEW YORK

Current Balance: $5,246,693.42

RECENT TRANSACTIONS

Nov 3, The Grand Regency (Presidential Suite–29 Days)
-$46,620.00

Nov 3, The Grand Regency (Capital Suite–29 Days)
-$39,720.00

Nov 3, The Grand Regency (Deluxe Room–29 Days)
-$22,620.00

Nov 3, Shiny and New Car Wash   -$99.00

Chapter $12

WEDNESDAY, NOVEMBER 3

Benji

Benji's parents were not impressed by the Presidential Suite. He even generously offered them the bigger of the two bedrooms. They only wanted to know the cost.

"I rented it for the month and got a great deal," he said. "Just a couple thousand bucks. That's nothing." He rounded down—way down. So basically, he lied.

"Oh, Benji, that's a waste," his mom said, and his dad mumbled under his breath.

Benji shrugged. "I thought this would be a nice surprise for you guys. They have a spa that will cover you in mud. And while we stay here, you can get the floors at home redone and the downstairs bathroom remodeled. Mom, you keep talking about it."

She heavy-sighed.

"Felix prepaid for it all, so we can't get our money back."

He didn't mean to blame Felix, but he knew it would shorten the lecture.

"You need to talk to us before making big decisions," his dad said.

Benji was quickly realizing that millions of dollars didn't really give a twelve-year-old independence. Parents were still ultimately in charge.

"It's not like I bought the hotel. It's just a room." He gave them his most charming smile, which had worked better when he had missing teeth and dimples than now with braces and pimples.

"Maybe the timing will work out," his mom said. "I'll talk to the contractor tomorrow."

Then they went to the hotel restaurant for dinner, where they argued over who would pay the bill. Benji lost the battle and didn't get to pick up the hundred-dollar tab. He also didn't get to order what he wanted. His mom made him get roasted chicken and a plain baked potato.

Now Benji lay on his hotel bed and worried that his parents were going to ruin this for him. He dug out his iPad to do some damage control.

November 3

You're not going to believe this. I'm a millionaire! Laura Friendly gave Felix and me five million dollars. It's so, so awesome but also very complicated because Felix and I have to share the money. We decided to get rooms at a hotel for about a month so we can figure things out, like how to buy stocks and invest wisely.

I went to school today, and that was fine. Then I went to open gym to play basketball, and that was great. I still don't know if I'll make the team. But I really want to, and I will try my best.

Also, Felix adopted a stray dog. I've always wanted a dog. Maybe I should get one too. I'm off to do homework.

Over and out,

Benji

Homework could wait. Benji wanted to do something fun—he needed to. He decided to visit Felix. Honestly, Felix wasn't much fun, not like his other friends. If anyone else was his co-millionaire, they'd probably be in California right now, riding roller coasters and eating corn dogs. But Felix was close by, just one floor below.

Benji slid on his shoes and got into the elevator. When the doors opened on the fourteenth floor, Felix stood there in red shorts, a Nintendo T-shirt, and hotel slippers. He must have gone home to get clothes and stuff. Freebie barked hello.

"Hey," Benji said. "Were you coming to see . . . Where are you going?"

"The pool." Felix stepped into the elevator.

"Me too."

"Really?" Felix asked, staring at Benji's outfit—joggers, a hoodie, and Converse.

"Yeah." Benji didn't have a bathing suit with him, but he was a millionaire—if he wanted to swim in his underwear, who could stop him?

Benji, Felix, and Freebie had the jelly bean–shaped pool to themselves. Wicker chairs surrounded the sides, and each had a freshly folded towel waiting.

"We're not supposed to be here. It says minors need to be accompanied by adults." Felix pointed to a giant sign on the wall. "We're breaking most of these rules. No pets. No minors. Shower before entering. Swimwear only."

"Relax, buddy. We're just *bending* the rules."

"Breaking," Felix insisted. "Maybe we should leave."

Benji made a sputtery sound. "Geez. Look at it this way. If you add our ages together, we're not minors; we're one adult. Freebie isn't a pet. He's a hotel guest and family member. And I showered after basketball."

"I don't know."

While Felix contemplated having fun, Benji pulled off his sweatshirt and his joggers. Then he jumped into the pool quickly so he wouldn't be standing on the deck in his boxer shorts. Benji didn't dive. It was one of the few rules he obeyed.

"Are you going to make me bend the rules alone?" he asked when he reemerged.

Felix secured Freebie's leash to one of the chairs. The dog pulled against it, trying to get to the pool.

"He wants to swim. Let him," Benji said.

"No." Felix stared at Benji like he'd said something offensive. "He might drown."

"Dogs are born knowing how to swim," Benji said, assuming it was true. He'd seen plenty of dog-in-water pictures and even a dog on a surfboard. "It's why they call it the doggy paddle. They do it naturally."

Felix took off the T-shirt and folded it. Then he kicked off his hotel slippers and put them neatly under the chair.

"Feel free to fold and iron my clothes, if you want," Benji joked.

Felix chewed on his thumbnail, ignoring Benji's comment. It was easy to tell when the kid was making a decision. Finally, Felix nodded and unclipped Freebie's leash.

"Do you want to swim, Freebie? Do ya?" Felix sang in a voice meant for babies and dogs.

Freebie answered by running and diving into the water. Felix jumped in right behind him, ready to rescue the dog.

"He'll be fine," Benji said.

Freebie splashed and basically swam in circles. But he didn't go under or drown.

"Here, boy," Felix called to the mutt.

Freebie's brown-and-gray head stuck out of the water like he was sniffing at the ceiling. His form was horrible, but he eventually made his way to Felix, who rewarded him with a hug and gave him a break from frantic paddling.

"My turn," Benji said. "Here, Freebie. Here, boy." Freebie turned and doggy-paddled in Benji's direction.

Suddenly, someone cleared their throat in that loud I-need-your-attention way. Benji turned to see a tall woman in a tan pantsuit staring down at them.

Uh-oh.

"Mr. Porter. Mr. Rannells. How is your stay so far?" She stood straight like a soldier.

"Great," Benji answered. "There's a TV over my bathtub."

Felix pulled Freebie to him and slowly moved behind Benji. Maybe he thought he could hide the dog.

"Wonderful. I'm glad you like your room." She gave a small nod. "It looks like you're also enjoying the pool."

"Yep."

"Unfortunately, we do not allow pets to use the pool." She tilted her head like she was delivering sad news. "However, since no other guests are using it this evening, we will make an exception. But please note that if there are any incidents with your dog . . ."

"Like if he poops or throws up?" Benji asked.

"Yes," the woman said. "We will have to charge your account for the cleanup."

"No problem," Benji said with a shrug.

"Thank you. I'd also like to remind you that the pool closes at nine and will reopen at eight a.m."

Benji looked at the massive clock on the wall. They still had over thirty minutes. "Okay."

"Can I do anything to make your stay more comfortable?" she asked, clasping her hands together.

"Can you order room service for me?" Benji asked. "Have it sent to my suite for nine, since we have to get out then anyway."

"Certainly. What would you like?"

"Everything."

"Everything?" she asked.

"Yes, two of everything. Please."

"I'll see to it, Mr. Porter. Have a good evening, Mr. Rannells." The woman smiled, nodded, and left.

"I don't know if I like being called Mr. Rannells," Felix said when the woman was gone.

"Right? Usually, when an adult calls me Mr. Porter, it means I'm in trouble." Then Benji put his hands together, creating a meaty rock, and splashed Felix and Freebie.

"But we didn't get in trouble." Felix splashed him back.

"Nope. Not yet."

Chapter $13

THURSDAY, NOVEMBER 4

Felix

A loud knock on the bedroom door woke Felix. He rubbed his eyes and for a moment didn't know where he was. Then he remembered. He was in the second-nicest suite at the Grand Regency, and he was a millionaire—for the month.

Freebie jumped off the bed and let out an annoyed bark.

"Felix, are you up?" his mom shouted through the door. "We need to leave in ten minutes."

"I'm up." He accidentally knocked his binder onto the floor. He'd fallen asleep without finishing his math homework.

After swimming, Felix had hung out in Benji's suite, eating room service and playing video games on their phones until after midnight. They'd spent a small fortune on in-app purchases: skins and maps in *Minecraft,* V-Bucks in *Fortnite,* unlimited lives and gems in a new multiplayer world-building game. In all, $12,600.

Felix pulled on a pair of jeans and a hoodie and then led Freebie out of the bedroom. He struggled to get the leash on the bouncing dog.

"You were up late last night," his mom said. "We need to set some rules."

"Okay." Though Felix did not need any more rules in his life.

"We'll talk later. That dog is about to stain the rug."

When he opened the door, he saw Benji and Reggie coming down the hallway.

"Morning, buddy!" Benji yelled. He carried a paper cup with steam drifting from the top. "Ready to go?"

"Almost."

Felix's mom stepped into the hall behind him. "What's going on?" Then she turned to Reggie. "Who are you?"

"Reggie Fazil, ma'am." He gave her a big smile and a slight bow before offering a handshake. "I'm their chauffeur."

Freebie jumped up, putting his paws on Reggie's chest.

"And dog-sitter," Reggie added as he let Freebie kiss his cheek.

"What?" Felix's mom looked to Felix for an explanation. "You hired a chauffeur?"

"Don't worry, Ms. Rannells," Benji said. "My parents ran a background check on Reggie last night. He's a good guy. He's got a clean driving record and has never been arrested."

"How old are you?" Felix's mom asked.

"Twenty-two, ma'am. I'm a student at the University at Albany. Chauffeuring and dog-sitting are not my long-term aspirations."

"He's studying philosophy," Felix added because it sounded important.

"More money in chauffeuring and dog-sitting," she mumbled. "I don't like what's going on here." She blinked a lot, and Felix knew that meant she was not happy.

"Wait. I know." Felix had an idea, and he wasn't sure if it was brilliant or ridiculous. "We could hire you, Mom. You can drive us around and we'll pay you."

"Whoa, am I being fired on my second day?" Reggie pulled his chin to his chest.

"Maybe we should talk about this." Benji grabbed Felix's sleeve.

"No. No." His mom wagged her finger. "You don't pay your mother to drive you around. I am not your employee. Not now. Not ever."

"Phew." Reggie laughed.

"Okay," Felix said, now knowing it wasn't a brilliant idea. "Um . . . I have to take the dog out, and then I'll just ride with them." He hoped his mom would allow it so he could finish his homework in the car.

"Fine." She went back into the room.

"We'll be in the car," Benji added. "Hurry up."

It was ten to eight when Felix and Freebie finally jumped into the empty backseat.

"We're going to be late," Felix said. "Sorry. It's my fault."

"No sweat." Benji turned in the front seat to talk to Felix. "If we're going to be late, we should really be late. Let's get doughnuts."

"You got it. What's your pleasure? Dunkin'?" Reggie asked.

"No, we have to get to school," Felix said.

"We will. Eventually." Benji nodded at Reggie. "Dunkin' is fine."

Felix hated to be late for school (though it wasn't something he'd ever actually done). But with or without stopping, they were going to miss the first bell. "If we're going to get doughnuts, we should go where my sister works. Downtown Donuts."

"You got it, boss." Reggie tapped on his phone and brought up a map.

Felix fished out his math notebook and started calculating angles on triangles, while Freebie tried to bite his pencil.

"Someone didn't do their homework," Benji sang.

"Did you?"

"No, but I have a special class second period where I get help with my work." Benji never seemed to worry about anything. He was the type of guy who just expected every-thing to work out. And it probably did for him.

Reggie pulled into a space in front of Downtown Donuts and offered to wait in the car with Freebie.

"Do you want anything?" Benji asked as he got out.

"Does Schopenhauer want a solution to human suffer-ing?" Reggie replied.

"Er . . . I have no idea," Benji said.

"He does." Reggie laughed. "And I'll take a Boston cream. If they've got 'em."

The bell over the door chimed as they walked in.

"Welcome to Downtown Do—" Georgie gave Felix a sideways glare. "Shouldn't you be in school?" She'd always straddled the line between sister and second mother. From as early as he could remember, she'd babysat for him, made him food, and read him stories. She'd also taught him to ride a bike and shoot a lay-up. She'd even forged his mom's signature on permission slips—not to be sneaky but be-cause their mother was busy doing the work of two parents.

"On our way," Felix said. Then he introduced Benji.

"So you're the co-millionaire," Georgie said.

"For now," Benji said with a shrug.

"What can I get you?" Georgie pointed a warning finger at Felix. "And it's not on the house this time." She'd often give him "free" doughnuts. They weren't exactly free; she just paid for them with her employee discount.

"All of it," Benji said.

"Sure." Georgie rolled her eyes and shook her head.

Felix got the impression that Benji wasn't joking.

"Whatever you got made, we'll take." Benji rested his hands against the glass counter. "All the doughnuts and fritters and sticky buns."

Georgie looked at Felix, and he nodded.

"We need to bring snack to school." He sounded like they were in kindergarten and today was his birthday.

"Okay." Georgie grabbed a box. "Chris, can you help me pack up *the store*?"

Benji took a seat while they waited for their order, and Felix opened the banking app. They weren't far off their daily target, but that was because they'd prepaid the hotel rooms.

FIRST BANK OF NEW YORK

Current Balance: $5,231,082.54

RECENT TRANSACTIONS

Nov 4, The Grand Regency (Room Service)   −$1,010.88

Nov 3, App Store   −$12,600.00

Nov 3, To: Reggie Fazil (Payroll–Dog-Sitting) −$1,000.00

Nov 3, To: Reggie Fazil (Payroll–Chauffeur) −$1,000.00

"We need to concentrate on spending," Felix whispered, not wanting Georgie to hear.

"Does this mean you're ready to quit school and focus on our problem?" Benji did air quotes around the word *problem.*

"No! But this weekend, we need to really spend money."

Benji nodded thoughtfully. "I hear Japan is expensive. Let's go there."

"I don't have a passport," Felix said.

"Okay. How about the next-best Japan? The one in Epcot."

"Disney?" Felix asked. "I've never been."

"You won't be able to say that on Monday." Benji snapped and pointed at Felix.

Could they really just go to Florida for the weekend? Didn't people plan for years to take a big trip like that?

"Hey, millionaires. Your order is ready. That'll be $516.70." Georgie put her hands on her hips. "Are you sure you want to do this? Even five million isn't going to last forever."

"I'm sure." Felix bristled. She was treating him like a baby, not just a baby brother. "And we'll be doing this every day. But a bigger order. One hundred and twenty dozen. Delivered." If Benji could buy pizza lunches for the school, he could buy doughnuts.

"I'm sure teachers are going to love that. A sugar rush

on top of the hormonal mood swings of middle schoolers."
She handed him a receipt.

Felix signed it and added a $103 tip—the amount Mr.
Trulz would approve. Georgie winked at him and smiled
when she saw it. If Felix had a choice, he'd have given his
sister ten thousand. But he had five million and few choices.

"Can I do anything else for you?" she asked.

"Yeah, can you take this weekend off?"

"Why?"

"Because we're going to Disney World."

Chapter $14

Benji

Benji and Felix set up the boxes of doughnuts near the cafeteria entrance. They had five minutes before the start of second period.

"Help yourself. Free doughnuts," Benji said to every kid who passed by, and most stopped and took at least one.

Then Alma Miranda walked up the hallway, singing silently. She wore her usual black T-shirt and jeans, and her hair was done up like Princess Leia. Did she know Benji had a crush on Princess Leia? *No way.*

"Doughnuts." He gestured at the boxes. "What kind do you like? I bet we got your favorite. We bought out the whole store."

"I like glazed." She smiled.

"We definitely have those." A warm sensation ran over Benji from head to toe that he couldn't explain.

"But I'm not hungry. I ate breakfast at home." She kept walking. "Oatmeal."

"Blech," he said.

"And half a cinnamon bun," she called over her shoulder. "So I'm good."

Benji stood in the middle of the hallway. "No normal person turns down pizza *and* doughnuts!"

She pivoted. "What's normal?"

"Um . . ." He could tell this was a trap. "Eating pizza and doughnuts is normal."

"Why do you get to decide what's normal?" She put a hand on her hip and stared at him. He didn't want to look away, but her eyes seemed to shoot lasers. She might blind him.

"I didn't mean . . . I just . . ." He wiped his sweaty hands on his jeans.

Suddenly, her serious, scary face broke into a smile. "I'm joking with you, Benji. I mean, you really shouldn't tell people what's normal and what's not. But I just don't want a doughnut right now. Don't take it personally, okay?"

"Okay. Does that mean you'll want a doughnut someday?" What was he saying? Was he asking her on a date? No! That was not what he was doing. Maybe it was. *Stop thinking, Benji!*

"Hey, that's not a bad idea," she said, and he almost fell over. "I'm on the committee—well, I *am* the committee—to organize the drama club fundraiser, and we need food for the event. If you wanted to donate food—"

"Yes!" he shouted, not bothering to consider if it was allowed by the rules before answering. "I mean, maybe. Probably. When is it?"

"December first or second, or maybe the third." She smiled again and rolled her eyes in the cutest way possible. "I'm waiting for Mr. Palomino to give me a date."

"If it's December first, I can hook you up."

"Why the first?" Her eyes searched his face for an explanation, and he had to turn away.

"I'm moving to Tibet after that." He lied, but he lied big enough that it wasn't just a lie, it was a joke. "So if you want doughnuts or pizza or anything else for your event, it's gotta be on the first."

The bell rang for their next class.

"Okay. I'll see what I can do." She waved goodbye.

• • •

After basketball, Benji walked to Reggie's car, while Felix ran.

"Hey, boy!" Felix said as he pulled open the car door. "I missed ya." Felix and Freebie fell all over each other. It was embarrassing, and yet Benji felt a little jealous.

"You guys stink," Reggie said. "Where to? The hotel, I hope. You need showers."

"Yeah." Benji sat in the front and put his forehead against the window to cool off.

"Everything good, boss?"

Benji shrugged. "Today was rough." More kids had shown up at open gym than ever, and some of them were good—really good. Benji had never been the best, but he'd always been the biggest. Now he worried that might not be enough.

"When are tryouts?" Reggie asked.

"Monday the fifteenth," Felix answered quickly.

"You guys going to make the team?"

"Maybe," Felix said.

Maybe? Benji already knew Felix wasn't a look-on-the-bright-side kind of guy. But this was an easy question. Felix was one of the top players in the school. The *maybe* was meant for Benji.

He turned around in the seat. "You don't think I'll make it?"

"I didn't say that."

"We know *you'll* make it," Benji continued. "So give it to me straight, Felix. Am I going to make the team?"

Felix looked stunned, like the question didn't make sense. "It's not up to me."

"Duh. I know that. What are my chances?" Benji motioned with his hands like he was weighing something.

Felix shrugged.

"Ugh!" Benji flopped back in his seat. "Why can't you just tell the truth?"

"Hmmm, truth," Reggie said. "Is there a greater pursuit than the search for truth? It's a central pillar of philosophy."

"I don't care about philosophy." Benji put his hands over his eyes and pressed hard. "I care about making the team."

"Felix cannot tell you if you'll make the team. An assertion can only be true or false in the past or present. Anything in the future is technically indeterminate."

Benji groaned. "Then how about an opinion."

"Opinions have little to do with truth," Reggie said. "They rely on our experiences and ingrained biases."

Benji couldn't imagine telling his parents that he hadn't gotten a spot. They'd sent him to basketball camp at Duke and at Syracuse. He'd played on teams at the YMCA since he was four. If he wasn't a basketball player, what would he be? He'd tried football but hated tackling other players. And that was all the coaches wanted him to do.

"Well." Benji faced Felix again. "I think you'll make the team. I think you'll be a starter."

"I hope so." Felix pulled at the sole of his right shoe. It opened like the lower jaw of an alligator.

"Felix, you're a millionaire. Why are you still wearing sneakers with holes?" Benji was done talking about basketball and his slim chances of making the team. That was a future problem. He put a hand on Reggie's shoulder. "Let's go shopping."

"Okay, boss," Reggie said. "But I still think you should shower first."

"Thanks for the advice," Benji said. "But when you have money, it doesn't matter if you smell. They'll just call us stinking rich."

Reggie took them to a sporting-goods store. Benji grabbed a cart and led them to the sneaker section. Rows of shoes lined the shelves, and a painted track on the floor circled the entire department.

"I want to see these, and these, and these, and these." Benji grabbed an armful of shoes and handed them to a guy with a name tag that read MIKE. "Size ten."

"Same for me, but in size six." Felix pulled Freebie away from a display of socks, but not before the dog snagged a pair in his mouth.

Mike returned with five boxes for Benji and only one for Felix. "Sorry, not all of them come that small."

"It's fine." Felix slowly opened the lid of his Nike Air Flight 89s and lifted the white-and-red high-tops out of the box like they were eggs. He ran a finger over the swoosh, fiddled with the laces, and then finally put one on. Fireworks practically shot out of his ears. It reminded Benji of the scene in *Cinderella* when Prince Charming put the glass slipper on her foot.

"They're perfect," Felix said.

Benji didn't bother trying his on and just dumped them in the cart.

"What else do we need?" he asked.

"I'd recommend foot powder and strong deodorant," Reggie said.

Benji ignored the suggestion and drove the cart like a scooter, going full-speed down the aisles. He hopped off at the Under Armour shirts.

"White or black?" he asked Felix.

"Um . . . black."

"Aaaint!" Benji made a buzzer sound. "That was a trick question. You want both." Benji tossed the shirts to Felix. Then he moved from rack to rack, grabbing any extra-small items for Felix and larges for himself: hoodies, sweatpants, tanks, T-shirts in every style and every color.

A few employees crept around, watching their shopping spree. Benji gave Mike a cheesy smile when he caught him snapping pictures.

"Take this." He rolled the cart to Felix. "I'll get another." Benji ran to the front. When he returned, Freebie had a half-deflated soccer ball in his mouth.

"Jersey time," Benji said. "What do you want?"

"All of them!" Felix was finally getting it.

In less than an hour, they'd filled three carts with gear, clothes, and shoes. The total came to $15,579.69.

"Nice work, buddy." Benji gave Felix a high five.

"This is the first time I've ever liked shopping." Felix smiled.

They pushed the carts to the Volkswagen. Reggie's

trunk wasn't big enough for their haul, and they had to put
some of the bags into the backseat.

"I think we're done for the day," Reggie said, trying to
close the trunk.

"Nah." Benji smiled. "I think we just need a bigger car."

FIRST BANK OF NEW YORK

Current Balance: $5,211,801.65

RECENT TRANSACTIONS

Nov 4, Big John's Sporting Goods	−$15,579.69
Nov 4, Little Italy Pizza and Pasta	−$3,080.00
Nov 4, Downtown Donuts	−$619.70
Nov 4, Vending Machine	−$1.50

Chapter $15

FRIDAY, NOVEMBER 5

Felix

It had taken twenty-four hours for Capital District Luxury Auto Rental to get the cars Felix and Benji wanted. In stock, they mostly had four-door sedans made by Lexus, BMW, or Mercedes. That wasn't going to cut it. And while Benji had clearly said they needed a bigger car, three of the four vehicles they rented were smaller than Reggie's Volkswagen.

"How am I supposed to drive four cars back to the hotel?" Reggie asked.

"I'll drive the Bugatti," Benji said.

"Sir." The serious salesman looked at Reggie. "Please do not let the children drive the vehicles."

"I'm not their guardian, but, ya know, I'll encourage them to follow the law." Reggie gave the salesman a big goofy grin and turned to Benji and Felix. "No driving. Don't do drugs. And you can't run for president until you're thirty-five."

Benji saluted. "Yes, sir."

"And the dog cannot—"

"Whoa!" Felix cut off the salesman. "He's gotta be over sixteen in dog years. He's totally getting his license and driving the Lamborghini."

The salesman did not laugh, but he did smile when Felix and Benji gladly paid for the extra insurance. A lot of it! They rented a black Porsche Taycan Turbo for *only* $549 per day plus insurance. The school-bus-yellow Lamborghini Urus cost $1,699 per day plus insurance. The silver-and-black Bugatti Veyron was the most expensive at $20,000 per day, plus a $100,000 security deposit, plus a $60,000 delivery fee (the dealer had brought it in from Miami), plus insurance.

But Felix's favorite vehicle was the cheapest—a fully loaded silver Range Rover. It had a huge moon roof, heated and massaging seats, and plenty of room for Freebie, and it cost a mere $350 per day, plus insurance.

"You sure you need four cars?" Reggie asked as they sat in the office, waiting for Mr. Trulz to handle the finance part.

"You only live once." Benji opened a can of Coke and raised it in a lone toast.

"Well, Aristippus would agree with that," Reggie said. "A very hedonistic approach to life."

"I know I shouldn't ask, but what are you talking about?" Benji said.

"A hedonist seeks joy and pleasure in life above all else. Aristippus was one of the first to embrace this thinking. He was a Grecian who loved to shop. His motto was basically 'The person who dies with the most stuff wins,'" Reggie explained.

"Cool motto. We should put it on a bumper sticker." Benji held his hands in front of him like he was imagining the final product.

Felix knew being called a hedonist wasn't a compliment. When the game was over, he promised himself to be the opposite of a hedonist. Whatever that might be.

The salesman returned with four sets of keys. "Which one is the winner? Which are you driving home?"

"The Bugatti!" Benji yelled.

"It only has two seats," Reggie reminded him.

For a minute, Felix thought Benji might suggest leaving Felix at the car dealership so he could ride in the Bugatti. He didn't. And together, they chose the Range Rover.

"We'll have the other vehicles and your Volkswagen delivered," the salesman said, and with the paperwork and payment taken care of, they left.

"Where to?" Reggie asked.

Benji turned in the front seat. "Felix, can we make a stop on the way to the hotel?"

"Um . . . sure." Felix wasn't used to Benji asking for his permission. This was new and a little worrisome.

"And do you mind if I invite someone else to go with us to Disney this weekend?" *Another question.* Maybe Benji was asking because he didn't know what to do for a change.

"I don't care. Who?" The guest list already included Felix's mom, Georgie and Michelle, Benji's parents, and of course, Reggie.

"Alma Miranda," Benji mumbled, and then turned up the car radio as if to end the conversation. But this didn't work because the Range Rover had a volume control in the back, too.

"Alma? Really? Do you like her?"

"Never mind." Benji blared the radio again, and Felix noticed the back of his neck turning red.

Felix turned off the music. "Yeah, let's invite her. You want to do it in person? Do you know where she lives?"

Benji mumbled a street address to Reggie and didn't say another word for the ten-minute drive. Felix enjoyed watching Benji fidget and look uncomfortable. Then he felt a little guilty for enjoying it.

When they pulled up to the house, Benji still didn't move or speak. Reggie glanced back at Felix. They both shrugged and tried not to laugh.

"Benji? Are you going to ask her?" Felix finally broke the silence. He couldn't sit here all night. He'd told his mom he'd be back by six.

"Can I borrow Freebie?" Benji flipped down the visor and checked his hair in the mirror. "Girls like dogs."

"Sure." Felix handed over the leash, but Benji still didn't move. "Want me to go in with you?"

"Yes!" And with that, Benji threw open the door and stepped out. Freebie hopped over the seat to follow.

"Be right back," Felix said to Reggie.

They walked onto the porch of a single-story house. Freebie sniffed every corner, and Felix waited for Benji to press the doorbell. But a bird flew out of the eaves before he got a chance, and Freebie went wild.

A second later, the wooden door opened, and Alma and an older girl stood behind the screen door.

"What are you doing here?" Alma asked.

"Do you know them?" The older girl had shoulder-length dark hair, huge brown eyes circled in black, and fire-truck-red lips that were hard to look away from.

"Yeah. That's Benji, and that's Felix. We go to school together, and they're the kids—"

"—who won the five million dollars." The girl pushed open the screen door. "Hi, I'm Ava. Alma's big sister. You guys want to come in?"

"Sure," Felix answered. He grabbed the center of Freebie's leash and pulled both the dog and Benji inside.

The house was neat and small and smelled like cinnamon. Ava led them to the kitchen and offered them still-warm cookies. Felix sat at the table, which was covered in homemade drama club posters.

"So, what's it like to be a tween millionaire?" Ava hopped onto the counter.

"It's good," Benji said. "Super cool. Really awesome."

"Impressive communication skills. You should write poetry." Ava laughed.

Alma sat cross-legged on the floor and patted her thigh to get Freebie's attention. The dog jumped into her lap. Alma smiled, though Freebie almost knocked her over.

"What about you, Felix?" Ava asked.

"It doesn't seem real yet," Felix said. "I keep imagining it's all going to go away."

"Well, it's not going to last forever if you keep buying pizza and doughnuts every day," Alma said, rubbing Freebie's belly.

"The food doesn't cost that much." Benji stood awkwardly in the middle of the kitchen. "And some kids like pizza. I like pizza. Pizza's good. Yummy."

They all stared at Benji.

"And why are you here?" Alma asked again.

"We're . . . um . . ." Benji struggled to speak, and Felix motioned for him to continue. "We're inviting some friends to go to Disney World with us?"

"Seriously?" Ava asked.

"We're going tomorrow," Benji continued. "Just for the weekend."

"I'll go," Ava said, raising her hand. "Take me. I'll be your friend. Your best friend."

"How are you getting there?" Alma asked.

"Private jet, of course," Benji said with a strange, almost British accent.

"That's got to be ridiculously expensive." Alma nudged Freebie off her lap and stood up.

"It's not a problem for us." Benji smiled. "We're millionaires. We can do what we want."

Felix ran a finger against his throat, trying to give Benji the quit-it sign. He was saying all the wrong things and didn't seem to realize it.

"If you can do anything you want, shouldn't you do something good? Do something big and important with your money?" Alma asked.

"We've rented a Bugatti," Benji said suddenly. "It's being delivered to the hotel."

Felix groaned to himself. This was not what Alma meant by big and important.

"What's a Bugatti?" Alma asked.

"An outrageously expensive car," her sister answered. "Maybe the most expensive in the world."

"Why would you do that?" Alma asked.

"It's a cool car?" Benji answered, but it came out like a question.

"Why do you need a cool car? You can't even drive."

"We have a driver."

"How much does a Bugatti cost?" Alma pulled her lips into a tight line.

Benji shrugged. "Don't remember."

She turned to Felix. "How much? And don't say you don't remember. We're in the same social studies class. You were the first to recite the preamble perfectly. You have an excellent memory."

"Um . . . we're only renting it."

"How much?"

"About twenty thousand." Felix didn't mention that was the cost per *day*, not the total bill, and didn't include insurance and security deposits.

Ava swore.

Benji opened his mouth wide in mocking surprise. "That can't be right."

"That's a huge waste of money," Alma said.

"What would you do with the money?" Benji asked. "Adopt orphans? Plant a forest?"

Alma narrowed her eyes at Benji. "Maybe. I'd have to think about it."

"You don't understand what it's like," Benji said.

"To be a millionaire? You're right. I don't."

"It's complicated. You're not in our shoes."

"Exactly. And how much did *those* cost?" She pointed at his Nikes.

"This is getting awkward." Ava stood up. "I'll be in my room. But just to be clear, I'm down with Disney if that's still an option."

"We're not going to Disney with them, Ava."

Benji's face turned pink, and his eyes looked watery. "Alma Miranda, you're very judgey. You hardly know me, and everything I do is wrong." Then he left.

"I'm not judgey," Alma said to Felix, who was the only one still in the kitchen.

"You're not *that* judgey," Felix said, trying to make her feel better.

"Gee, thanks."

"You can't understand what it's like for us. For Benji. Or for me."

"Don't ask me to feel sorry for a couple of millionaires." She crossed her arms and slumped against the wall.

"No. I don't think anyone will ever feel sorry for us. But it's complicated." There was no way to explain. Benji and Felix looked like selfish jerks to everyone. And there was nothing they could do to change that until after December 1.

FIRST BANK OF NEW YORK

Current Balance: $4,396,746.29

RECENT TRANSACTIONS

Nov 5, Capital District Luxury Auto Rental
(Bugatti Veyron [rental/tax/ins/dlvr/dep])   −$727,000.00

Nov 5, Capital District Luxury Auto Rental
(Porsche Taycan [rental/tax/ins])   −$17,523.00

Nov 5, Capital District Luxury Auto Rental
(Lamborghini Urus [rental/tax/ins])   −$51,273.00

Nov 5, Capital District Luxury Auto Rental
(Range Rover [rental/tax/ins])   −$11,475.00

Chapter $16

SATURDAY AND SUNDAY, NOVEMBER 6 AND 7

Benji

Benji looked around the private plane and smiled. He'd made this happen, with the help of a travel agent named Betsy. He'd told her to spare no expense. A phrase he'd learned from movies—well, a movie, *Jurassic Park*.

The plane was gorgeous—white leather, polished wood, and shiny metal. Benji had never been on Air Force One, but he imagined this was just as awesome. And the only way this mini-vacation could have been better was if Alma had been here. Or, she could have at least been nicer when Benji offered her a free trip.

"You okay?" Felix asked. He sat on the far side of the couch from Benji. Freebie lay between them. The dog seemed to consider himself human.

"I'm great! We're going to Disney!" Benji said, a bit too excitedly. "I still can't believe you've never been. I've gone like a dozen times."

"Plenty of people have never been to Disney World. It's over seven hundred miles away and expensive."

Benji's parents and Ms. Rannells sat around the table in the back, drinking cups of coffee. Benji couldn't hear their conversation over the hum of the engines, but they smiled and nodded, so he imagined they were talking about the weather and not money. His dad didn't smile when talking about money.

"Anyone want to play Uno?" Reggie asked.

"No, thanks," Georgie replied. She shared a chair that was meant for one with her fiancée, Michelle. They whispered to each other with foreheads touching. Benji thought if the plane hit turbulence, they'd probably knock each other out. He'd never seen anyone so in love—except maybe Felix with Freebie.

Benji, Felix, and Reggie played Uno until the plane touched down in Florida at 10:00 a.m. Waiting at the airport were two black SUVs with Disney logos, and thirty minutes later, they pulled up in front of the Magic Kingdom.

A guide in a plaid vest promised them the most magical day of their lives. Benji had booked VIP packages, which allowed them to skip lines and do everything in a single weekend. Another employee collected Freebie for a day at the doggy spa.

"Where would you like to begin?" the guide asked.

"We'd like to go on the Dumbo ride. It's iconic. And the teacups. And to meet Mickey, of course," Georgie said. "But we can do that on our own. We can meet you later." She held Michelle's hand, and they swung their arms back and forth like little kids.

"I want to ride Dumbo," Felix said.

Benji couldn't suppress his groan. He wanted the big attractions—the faster, the louder, the higher, the better.

"What do you want to do?" Felix asked him.

"Anything," Benji said. "Everything." He'd just been to Disney over spring break last year. He'd ridden Dumbo, Splash Mountain, and every other ride in the park.

The guides led them to Dumbo, where they jumped ahead in line. Georgie and Michelle rode together. Benji's parents climbed into an elephant—his mom insisted they ride together, as if it was romantic. Ms. Rannells told Felix to go with his friend and she'd sit with Reggie.

"Okay," Felix said quickly, and ran to an empty elephant.

For a second, Benji felt like he should be embarrassed and should refuse to ride Dumbo, especially with someone else who was twelve. This was a three-year-old's ride. But no one knew him here—except the people he'd brought—and he hadn't flown three hours to watch other people have fun. He crawled in next to a smiling Felix.

This is cool as long as no one takes pictures.

Then Georgie twisted in her seat and snapped a picture on her phone.

"You guys are so cute," she said. "You're just missing a set of ears."

Benji hid his face.

The boys circled and soared on Dumbo. Felix held up his hands and screamed like it was the thrill of a lifetime. When the ride was over, Felix wanted to go again.

So they did. And this time, Benji screamed and held up his hands.

They spent the next two hours on the *basic* rides—the ones Benji would have preferred to skip. Then they headed to the bigger rides. The guide walked them to Space Mountain and the Runaway Train and Splash Mountain, where Benji got so wet, he might as well have swum through it. The parents kept up for a little while before they traded in rides for shows and food.

"We're going to wander on our own too," Georgie said to the group, but her eyes were focused only on Michelle. "We want to get our picture with Elsa."

"Sure," Benji said, not that they needed his permission.

Michelle turned to him and Felix, smiling. She was pretty, with brown eyes and straight black hair that came to a point at her chin. When she smiled, she looked like a model.

"Thank you both. We're having the time of our lives. We might not get a honeymoon right away, so this is a special trip. A pre-honeymoon." Michelle kissed Georgie on the cheek.

"You're welcome," Benji said proudly. Man, it felt good to do stuff for other people. He'd have bought them a honeymoon right then, but he knew the troll would say it was illegal. Unless he accompanied them, and nobody wanted that.

Benji, Felix, and Reggie spent a few more hours at the Magic Kingdom before heading over to Hollywood Studios, home of Star Wars: Galaxy's Edge. They rode all the major attractions, including the Rock 'n' Roller Coaster. It was one of the rides that snaps a picture at the most terrifying part. And their pic was the best photo ever. Every muscle in Felix's face and neck was clenched. Benji's mouth hung open in utter terror. And Reggie's man bun came undone, and he appeared to be crying. After that, Reggie called it quits and went to their hotel to do homework.

Felix and Benji stayed for fireworks and didn't leave until the parks closed. They'd booked four rooms at the most expensive hotel they could get on short notice. And on Sunday morning, they were the first in line to go back.

They rode all the best rides at each park. They bought Mickey ears and every *Star Wars*–themed item they came across, including creating their own droids. They ate the grey stuff, and it was, indeed, delicious. But at 5:00 p.m., they had to say goodbye to their vacation. They gathered Freebie from the luxury kennel, and their families headed back to their private jet.

On the plane ride home, everyone fell asleep after takeoff—except the boys. The cabin lights dimmed, and Benji and Felix sat at the small table close to the cockpit.

"Check out how much we spent." Felix, still wearing his Mickey ears, held up his phone for Benji.

"Yes!" Benji gave him a high five. "And it's been less than a week. We're ahead of schedule, and this trip was epic."

"This was probably the best weekend of my life." Felix pulled Freebie into his lap.

"Me too," Benji said.

"Really? You've been to Disney a million times," Felix said. "It's nothing special."

"This time was different." Benji shrugged.

"Because of the money?"

"An unlimited budget does have a way of making things better." Benji snorted. "But not just that. I'm an only child. I've never had a brother or anyone to hang out with on vacation. This was cool."

Felix nodded.

"I'm glad we're doing this together, buddy." Benji smiled and then leaned back in his chair and closed his eyes.

FIRST BANK OF NEW YORK

Current Balance: $4,290,347.56

RECENT TRANSACTIONS

Nov 7, Direct Connect Private Jets   −$76,000.00

Nov 7, Disney World (Merchandise)   −$1,310.09

Nov 7, Disney World (Admissions)   −$2,240.00

Nov 7, Disney World (Grand Floridian Resort and Spa)

−$7,537.52

Chapter $17

MONDAY, NOVEMBER 8

Felix

After school, Felix and Benji played basketball during open gym and then got busy doing their *real* work of spending money. Burning through hundreds of thousands of dollars was easier on the weekend than on a weekday. Still dressed in their sweaty gym clothes, they sat in the Presidential Suite, shopping online.

They made a game of it—each only had five minutes to make an expensive purchase. Felix had already ordered a computer, more sneakers, sunglasses, and a VR headset. He paid a little extra for overnight shipping on everything. Benji also got a second new computer, more sneakers, cowboy boots, and a drone.

"We've spent less than ten grand," Benji said as he handed the laptop to Felix. "We need to think bigger or we'll be here all night."

"You're right." Felix had been buying stuff he wanted, not focusing on the price and the end goal of spending every penny. He drummed his fingers on the keyboard.

"But you still only have five minutes," Benji said with a smile. "Go!"

"Okay. Okay." Felix Googled expensive dog stuff and found puppy perfume that cost three thousand dollars.

Click. Buy.

"Nice." Benji gave him a high five and took the laptop back for his turn. A moment later, Mr. Trulz called Benji's cell phone.

"Les Petites Puppies Perfume. Is that for you?" Mr. Trulz asked on speaker.

"Yes, I need it for my dog," Felix said. "He comes from the streets and smells like garbage sometimes." Not true. Freebie never smelled like garbage anymore.

"Carry on," Mr. Trulz said, and hung up.

"Score!" Benji yelled suddenly. "A vintage Hermès handbag for seventy-two thousand." As soon as he clicked the buy button, Mr. Trulz rang again. Benji assured him that the purse was for him and he would carry it proudly.

"You should buy a handbag too," Benji said, giving back the PC. "They're more expensive than sneakers."

"No, thanks." But Felix realized Benji was onto something with vintage—meaning old stuff. And what was older than fossils? He clicked through site after site until he found a one-of-a-kind purchase.

"Go ahead and declare me the winner, please." Felix turned the screen to show Benji. Felix was now the owner of a $250,000 T. rex skull.

"Oh my God, are there more?" The surprise on Benji's face turned to a giant, goofy smile. "Let's buy ten of them."

"No more tyrannosauruses, but they've got some smaller fossils."

The accountant called *again*. They argued briefly about whether the T. rex skull could be considered art. It was mounted on a beautiful marble base and belonged in a museum—a science museum, not an art museum.

"I'll allow it. Just one," Mr. Trulz warned.

"That's not fair," Benji whined. "I want a fossil too."

"Fine. One fossil each." So Benji ended up with a triceratops skull for $65,000.

"You're up." Benji handed the laptop to Felix, but their game was interrupted by knocking.

"Hey, Mom," Felix said, after he opened the door. "What are you doing here?" He tried to read her face. It didn't seem like he was in trouble.

"I want to have dinner with you and your sister," she said.

"Okay. Where do you want to go? My treat." He smiled and wriggled his eyebrows. She hadn't said much about the money or his spending, but she'd taken to heavy-sighing. A lot.

She pulled on the collar of her Express Services shirt and sighed as if on cue. "We're not going out. I'm cooking."

After Felix said goodbye to Benji and took a quick shower, his mom drove him and Freebie to the apartment in her Toyota. His mom had said she'd be cooking, but that didn't mean Felix didn't have to help. He sautéed onions and garlic in olive oil for marinara sauce. His mom mixed ground beef, spices, and bread crumbs for the meatballs. The apartment filled with delicious smells, and his stomach grumbled.

"How's school?" his mom asked as she formed the meatballs and lined them up on a cookie sheet.

"Fine."

"Are things different now?"

"Not really." In fact, they were very different. He used to feel invisible. Now it was like he wore an orange construction vest and carried those signaling flashlights they have at airports. Everyone knew his name and tried to talk to him (mostly asking him to buy them stuff). Just today, Luke and Jeremy had shown him a catalog with a three-thousand-dollar telescope. They wanted him to "donate" it to the science club.

"I don't believe you." She hip-checked him but didn't press.

Georgie arrived right as dinner was ready.

After they said grace, Felix took a massive scoop of spaghetti and poured a ladle of sauce on top. He grabbed only four meatballs but planned to go back for more.

"I need to talk to you both," his mom said with a smile.

"I want to go back to school for my nursing degree. I want to be an RN, and eventually get my master's."

"Why?" Georgie asked like she'd tasted something rotten.

"Excuse me?" His mom's smile faded.

"Why work at all?" Georgie said. "Your son's a millionaire."

His mom put down her fork. "I like working. I like helping people and having a purpose. My son may be a millionaire, but I'm not."

"Well, it would be easier to go back to school if you quit your jobs," Georgie said. "Let Felix give you money—or lend you money—for bills and insurance."

Shut up, Georgie. He wanted to kick her under the table, but she wouldn't understand why he needed her to be quiet. She was spouting bad ideas. Impossible ideas.

"Maybe I should quit my job too," Georgie continued. "I can go to culinary school. Maybe in Paris. Felix could support us all."

"Since when do you like cooking?" his mother asked. "I thought you dreamed of selling your own line of jewelry."

Georgie touched the silver necklace around her neck. She'd made it from antique spoons. "Dreams are for people with savings accounts."

"Mom," Felix said. "Are you quitting your job?" *She can't quit! What will we live on? I don't really have millions.*

"No, of course not. I'll keep working," his mother said.

"I think if we get a smaller apartment, we'll be fine. I've been considering this for a while."

Smaller? This place had one bedroom. He slept on a couch.

"I told the landlord we're not renewing our lease. We'll have to move out at the end of December."

Felix swallowed a meatball practically whole. It felt like a rock in his throat. They were going to end up homeless.

"Felix, you should buy a house," Georgie said.

I can't! He kept his eyes on the table.

Georgie and his mom argued about how Felix should spend or invest his money. He pushed the food around on his plate, trying to ignore them and sneaking bites of bread to Freebie.

"Felix? Are you all right?" His mom put her hand on his.

"Um . . ." He wanted to tell them the truth. That was the only thought that popped into his head. "Please just don't quit your job. Okay?"

"Don't worry. I'm not quitting. Let's talk about something else," his mom said, all cheery. "Any wedding plans?"

Georgie sighed. "Probably in the summer. We have to do it outside at a park or maybe Michelle's parents' backyard. We can't afford anything else, and we're saving for a house." She shot a look at Felix.

He couldn't buy her a house. He couldn't buy her a car. He couldn't buy her a T-shirt in Disney World over the weekend.

But he could buy her a wedding!

"I'll pay for your wedding." He leaned forward in his chair. "How much does a wedding cost?"

"Anywhere from a few thousand dollars to hundreds of thousands. Depends on where, the menu, the number of people, a lot of things. But Michelle and I don't need anything lavish."

"You could have your wedding at the Grand Regency. They have a nice ballroom, and the gardens outside are pretty. That's where Freebie goes to the bathroom, but I always pick it up."

"The Grand Regency is expensive, Felix," Georgie said, but she didn't say no.

"I know the manager. She'd probably give me a discount." He was definitely not going to ask for a discount.

"You think?" The sour look on Georgie's face was finally gone. But his mom looked like they were speaking in a different language and she didn't know what was happening.

"But you need to get married before the end of the month." Felix didn't think this was a big deal. They'd been engaged for over a year and lived together in a mobile home they rented from Michelle's grandfather. Seemed like they'd want to get married and get it over with.

"Why?" his mom asked. Her eyes narrowed, and he had to look away.

"Um . . . because we don't plan to live at the hotel forever." He forced a smile. "If we want to get a good deal, we need to move fast."

He could tell his mom wasn't buying it. Just like she knew school was not the same. But, again, she didn't push for answers.

"I'll have to ask Michelle. But why not? I want to be married, and I want you to walk me down the aisle, Felix." She reached across the table and squeezed his hand. "Traditionally, it's the father of the bride's job. But it's not like Mark is part of our lives."

Felix flinched. He couldn't remember the last time anyone had said their father's name out loud. They had an unspoken agreement: Don't mention or even think of him—their own he-who-must-not-be-named.

"It's sweet you want your little brother to walk you down the aisle," his mom said, ignoring the Mark mention. "But not sweet you want him to pay." She glared at him but didn't actually look upset.

"I'm happy to do both," Felix said. He took a bite of spaghetti. Seeing his mom and sister smile made his appetite come back.

Chapter $18

TUESDAY, NOVEMBER 9

Benji

A loud knocking woke Benji.

"What time is it?" he asked, pulling a blanket over his head.

The door cracked open and Felix answered, "Six. I'm skipping school and going to Boston. Will you cover for me?"

"What? You're bending a rule?" Benji sat up. "Why?"

Freebie pushed his way in and jumped on the bed.

"Laura Friendly is in Boston for the day, and I need to talk to her. I'm going to ask her to change one of the rules." Felix took a deep breath. "I can't keep this a secret. I have to tell my mom before she quits her job and gives up our apartment. She thinks I can buy us a house."

A rule change wasn't a bad idea. If Benji could tell his parents, maybe they'd stop lecturing him. At last night's dinner, all they'd talked about was lawyers and investments and responsibility. And they'd forced him to order healthy food.

"I'll go with you," Benji said.

"What are we going to do about our parents?" Felix asked.

"Nothing," Benji said. "They'll assume we went to school, and if it all goes well, we'll be home by dinner, and we can explain everything."

They met in front of the hotel at the usual leave-for-school time. Reggie didn't flinch at their instructions, but he did convince them to leave Freebie behind with the hotel manager, who promised to find a dog-sitter.

"By the way," Felix said after they piled into the Lamborghini Urus. "We're paying for my sister's wedding. It'll be next weekend at the hotel. You're both invited. Everyone's invited."

"I'll be there," Benji said.

"And you can bring a date," Felix said, and Benji's face warmed.

He tried to reply "Maybe," but it came out sounding like "Me-me." Then he pulled out his phone and pretended to be taking care of urgent business.

The ride to Boston took just under three hours. They probably could have made it in two if Reggie hadn't driven the Urus like an old lady.

"Come on, it's a sports car," Benji had begged.

"Yeah. Cops love to pull over sports cars," Reggie had replied.

Reggie dropped them in front of a skyscraper and told them to call when they were done.

At the tall desk in the lobby, Benji gave their names and asked to see Laura Friendly. The receptionist's reaction was as expected—raised eyebrows, shaking of the head, and pursed lips. But after a few phone calls, they were granted entry.

"Hello, Felix. Hello, Benji. Nice to see you again." Laura Friendly's assistant, Tracey, greeted them as they stepped out of the elevator on the twentieth floor.

"Hello," Benji replied.

"I know you want to speak to Laura, but she has a packed schedule today. I'll see what I can do." Tracey led them down a hallway past dozens of offices to a sleek conference room. The glass table was surrounded by black chairs that looked like they belonged on a spaceship. Two of the walls were windows that looked out onto a park and the water. Benji couldn't imagine anyone doing work in here—too distracting.

"Have a seat. I'll have some breakfast brought up." Tracey pulled the double doors closed as she left.

"I bet they make us wait all day. They'll keep telling us Laura Friendly is busy. And then at like five o'clock, they'll say she left town for some important business in Tokyo or something." Benji collapsed into one of the chairs and started spinning.

But before he made it through two complete rotations, Laura Friendly burst into the room wearing a reflective jogging suit that made her look like a small astronaut.

"Good morning, boys."

"Looks like you were wrong," Felix mumbled.

Laura Friendly took the seat closest to the door. Then she drank from a tall water bottle filled with a green liquid. There were jokes on the internet that claimed she wasn't human—maybe they weren't jokes.

"What can I do for my favorite temporary millionaires?" she asked.

"It's not going to be temporary," Benji replied.

"We'll see." She shook her drink.

It made sense that she didn't want them to succeed. It'd cost her twenty million. But Benji wondered if she would actually be happy to see them fail, like a truly evil villain.

"I need to ask you something," Felix said. "Would you consider changing the rules, please?"

"No."

"I just want to—"

"Felix. It is Felix, right?" She gestured between them. "I get the two of you confused."

Felix nodded.

"I cannot change the rules."

"I don't want to change *all* the rules," Felix tried to explain.

"No!" She placed both hands on the table.

"You didn't even hear which rule," Benji said, copying her posture. "Will you listen to him before you make up your mind?"

"I will not change the rules. But if you insist, you can tell me which one is an issue." She waved her hand as if to say "Get on with it."

"I just want to tell my mom about the challenge," Felix said quickly.

"She might quit her job," Benji added, talking much louder than Felix. "And she gave up their apartment."

Laura Friendly looked at Felix and then Benji and then Felix again. Her eyebrows arched up, and one side of her mouth pulled down. Maybe she had a heart after all.

"So, can I tell my mom?" Felix lowered his head.

"Not if you want to win," Laura Friendly answered.

"You're the worst!" The words came out of Benji's mouth before he had a chance to think about them. A common problem. For a second, he worried she would cancel the whole deal and kick them out. But she just laughed.

"You don't know the half of it." She stood and twisted, stretching her back. "Anything else?"

Felix shook his head. He looked paler than usual.

Laura Friendly finished the green sludge in her water bottle and turned toward the door.

"I have a question," Benji said. This wasn't planned; it just popped into his brain. "If you were us, how would you spend the money?"

"I'm not going to give you a solution," she said. "That's not playing fair."

"Why? It's not against the rules. We're just kids. We can't talk to anyone else." Benji shrugged.

"Plus, you're brilliant. I read your book," Felix said. "Even though you quit college, it wasn't because you weren't smart."

"I quit because I *was* smart." She put a finger to her chin. "How would I spend all that money quickly?" She seemed to be talking to herself. "I'd see the world. Singapore, Zurich, Melbourne. Oh, I know. You should visit Tuvalu. It's an island nation that's not going to be around long if oceans keep rising."

"I don't have a passport," Felix said.

"And we have school," Benji added. "It's basically a full-time job. We should actually be there now."

She laughed. "I don't miss being a child. Not at all." She glanced at her smartwatch. "I've reserved the executive gym. Care to join me?"

"Sure," Benji answered. "And being a kid isn't so bad. Except when you're being tortured by an evil billionaire."

"Don't think of it as torture. If you do it right, this month might be the highlight of your life."

Chapter $19

TUESDAY, NOVEMBER 9

Felix

"Hi, Mom," Felix said when her voice mail picked up. "I'm in Boston with Benji and Reggie and Laura Friendly. Don't worry. Everything is good. We had a business meeting. I just forgot to tell you." Felix's stomach hurt from the half lie. "The hotel manager has someone watching Freebie. Can you check on him and bring him to the room? I'll be home late. We're going to a Celtics game. Look for me on TV. Love you." He turned off his phone to save the battery—well, that was one of the reasons.

Turned out, Laura Friendly was a big basketball fan—Lakers fan, specifically. Over lunch in Boston Common, Felix learned she had season tickets in LA. She also liked skiing, had never played *Minecraft* until this afternoon, and always fell asleep at the opera. ("At least on eight occasions.") Felix, Benji, and Laura Friendly had spent the whole day together. Her assistant was not happy. From the sound of it, Laura Friendly had missed a hundred meetings and a thousand phone calls. All of which were extremely important and costly.

"Do you think we can get floor tickets?" Felix asked as Reggie drove them to the TD Garden.

"You don't want floor seats." Laura Friendly sat in the front, playing with the radio. "Players crash into the front row. You want a luxury box. Let me make a call."

"No! I want Carl Jones Moore to crush me," Felix said.

Laura Friendly clicked her tongue. "When you get a size-fifteen shoe in your face, you may think different."

"So, can we get front row?" Felix asked. No one was going to convince him those weren't the best seats.

"For the right price, you can get anything," Benji replied.

Laura Friendly groaned. "Common misconception."

"In modern society, scholars argue that money is a need like air, water, food, and shelter," Reggie added. "All citizens, all people, need access to money for survival."

"It's a means to get what you truly need." Laura Friendly seemed to enjoy arguing with everyone. "You cannot eat a dollar bill."

"Well, I'm not eating my money. I'm using it to buy primo seats, baby." Benji held up his phone, showing off the tickets—three rows back and almost midcourt. Close enough to get sweat flung on them.

Reggie parked the Lamborghini in a VIP lot for a hundred dollars. Laura Friendly tried to pay, but Benji beat her to it.

"Sorry," she said. "I forgot."

Before making their way to the seats, Benji and Felix stopped off at a merchandise stand.

"Two of everything," Benji said to the attendant.

"I'd buy you a Moore jersey," Felix said to Ms. Friendly. "But I'm not allowed."

"And I wouldn't wear it. Even if I was dead."

The foursome found their seats, but Felix didn't sit. He stood as the teams warmed up. He stood for the national anthem and the announcement of the starting lineup. He stood for the tip-off. He stood for the first five minutes of the game.

"Why did we buy seats if you weren't going to use them?" Benji asked.

Reggie, who declared he wasn't a sports fan, read a book by someone named Nietzsche. Laura Friendly criticized every play by *both* teams. And Benji was mostly interested in food: popcorn, nachos, fries, and hot dogs (which Felix refused out of guilt—he hadn't had a hot dog since the field trip—and Reggie refused because he was a vegetarian).

At the end of the first quarter, the Celtics were up by three. Felix finally sat in his seat and chugged a Coke, while Benji went to buy even more food.

"Having fun?" Ms. Friendly asked.

"This is . . . great." *Great* didn't begin to describe it. "I've never been to an NBA game."

"You should go to a Lakers game. *Those* are great."

"If I was a billionaire, I'd go to every Celtics game. And maybe I'd start following football and baseball, too."

"When you do something all the time, it loses its appeal. It's no longer special," Ms. Friendly said. "You need to pace yourself."

That was easy, ridiculous advice for a billionaire to spew. Plenty of people watched their team every time they played.

"You can have whatever you want and do anything you want. Maybe you shouldn't complain about that." He stared at his Air Flights, embarrassed about speaking to an adult that way. But she shouldn't act like money was a curse. It wasn't! Except when you had to spend five million in thirty days.

"There are limits to everything," she said, and Felix could sense she was staring at him.

"Not when you have billions."

"Billions can't buy another hour in the day. Can't even buy me an extra minute."

"But . . ." Felix looked up and raised a finger to stop her. "It can buy you a cook and a maid and someone to do all your work, which frees up time. That's like getting an extra hour."

"Not quite the same."

Felix just shrugged.

"And money can't buy a do-over." She sighed. "Can't rewind time and give you a second shot at something."

Felix's mind immediately flashed to the twenty dollars. They shouldn't have taken it, or at least, he should have returned the money the next day.

"That's what I'd buy if I could. A do-over." Laura Friendly nodded to herself. "I missed something important, and I'll never get that opportunity again. I want to do that day over. March twentieth. A year and a half ago."

Felix didn't get a chance to ask what had happened. The second quarter started, and Benji returned with ice cream and candy bars.

"I got a Crunch bar, Ms. Friendly. Didn't even have to steal it. Want some?" He broke it in half and offered her a piece.

"Thank you, Benji," she said, taking the chocolate.

In the second quarter, the Celtics went up by ten. With every basket, deafening cheers erupted from the crowd. The place vibrated. A player even crashed into the seats, and Felix got elbowed in the head. He hoped it would leave a bruise.

"Do you play basketball?" Ms. Friendly asked Benji at halftime while dancers took over the court.

"Yeah. So does Felix. We're trying out for the school team."

"But you're so small," she said to Felix. He knew this but still hated it when people pointed out the obvious.

FIRST BANK OF NEW YORK

Current Balance: $3,871,795.15

RECENT TRANSACTIONS

Nov 9, TD Garden Food Court	–$363.20
Nov 9, Celtics Fan Shop	–$2,135.00
Nov 9, TicketGrabber.com (Celtics vs. Mavericks)	
	–$7,200.00
Nov 9, TD Garden VIP Parking	–$100.00

"Don't let that fool ya," Benji said, coming to Felix's defense. "He's good. Really good."

When the dancing finished, the announcer explained some kind of shooting contest. Felix only half listened as a camera panned around the arena and stopped on contestants. Their faces were projected on the Jumbotron over the court.

Felix watched and wished the game would start again. Then he realized it was his face on the screen. Benji was the first to jump and yell like the world was on fire. Then Reggie and even Laura Friendly hooted.

"What's happening?" Felix felt heat rising up his neck.

"You're going to take the half-court shot!" Benji smacked Felix hard on the back and knocked him into the group of guys in front of them. They didn't seem to mind; they pushed Felix toward the aisle. Toward the court. Toward inevitable humiliation.

The crowd cheered as the three contestants made their way to the man with the mic. A young woman jogged to the center, pumping her fist over her head. An older guy who looked like he was hiding a basketball under his T-shirt came from the far bleachers. And Felix.

"Are you ready for a chance to win ten thousand dollars?" the announcer asked. The woman and the man and the crowd screamed yes.

"You get one shot," the announcer continued. "You must release the ball before the half-court line. If it goes in, you're ten thousand dollars richer, thanks to our sponsors at Crown Honda. Ladies first." The announcer asked her name.

"Bella," she said with a curtsy. Then she selected a ball from the rack and dribbled to the center circle. The crowd began chanting her name. Bella drew the ball back underhand and launched it like a softball pitch.

The ball sailed through the air and hit the backboard off-center.

The crowd gave a collective "Aw!"

The man offered to let Felix go next, but Felix shook his head. So the man grabbed a basketball. He started nearly at the opposite baseline and ran with the ball to center court, then flung the ball and himself. The ball sank well before the basket, and he landed on his knees.

Then it was Felix's turn.

He selected a ball from the rack. It felt soft, so he picked a different one. This made the crowd go "Oooooh" like Felix knew what he was doing. He walked to the center tip-off circle and dribbled the ball four times. The same routine he did before every foul shot—shots he often missed. And this was three times farther from the basket. He might as well have been on Mars.

He didn't want to attempt the shot.

· But he also really wanted to make the shot.

He couldn't do the second without the first.

The crowd chanted his name, and players began appearing from their locker room.

"Now or never, Felix," the announcer added.

So Felix did the only rational thing that would give him a chance of sinking a basket. He moved his legs wide, held the ball in two hands, and threw a potty shot.

The crowd laughed at first. But as the ball smoothly arced to the basket, the stadium quieted, and time slowed down. It hit the rim. Bounced gently off the backboard. Hit the rim again. And finally fell through the hoop.

Small fireworks erupted from the ceiling. The lights in the entire building turned green, and his name flashed on the scoreboard. A Celtics player—Felix was too disoriented to know which one—ruffled his hair.

"Felix! Felix!" The announcer could barely be heard over the crowd noise. "Congratulations! What are you going to do with the ten thousand?"

Felix shrugged. He'd just made the shot of a lifetime in front of thousands of people, and for the first time in a week, he actually hadn't been thinking about money.

"Um . . . I guess I can give it to my mom." With that realization, his night got even better.

Chapter $20

WEDNESDAY, NOVEMBER 10

Benji

When Benji walked into the hotel restaurant, he saw his parents, Felix and his mom, and Reggie seated in the corner. No one was eating.

Benji had only gotten four hours of sleep last night and didn't have the energy for a breakfast meeting, but his mom had insisted.

"Good morning." He forced cheeriness into his voice.

"We need to talk about your *field trip* to Boston," his mom said.

Benji held back a groan. Starting with "We need to talk" always meant "Benji, you need to listen."

"What made you think it was okay to skip school and leave town for an entire day without telling anyone?" she asked.

"It was a business trip." Benji looked to Felix for help, but Felix had gone into turtle-hiding-in-his-shell mode.

134

"You are not a CEO. You are not a businessman." His dad gripped the table.

"You are a twelve-year-old child," his mom said.

"Something could have happened to you," Ms. Rannells added. She ran a hand over Felix's red hair.

"Reggie was there," Benji said. "He's an adult."

"Man, don't pull me into this? I'm just the driver." Reggie held up his hands. "I go where I'm told."

"He's barely an adult." Benji's mom shook her head.

"He's twenty-two. He can vote and buy alcohol." Instantly, Benji realized that this was probably not the right thing to say.

"He is not your guardian," his mom said.

"We're sorry," Felix murmured. It seemed like his way out of every situation was to apologize. And by saying "we," he'd dragged Benji into the strategy.

"Mom, I can't explain everything right now," Benji said, decidedly not taking the apology route. "You've got to trust me. We needed to go to Boston. We'll make up the schoolwork. Everything is fine. I promise."

"Trust you?" his dad asked. "How much money have you spent so far?"

Ms. Rannells held up her hands. "No, no. We said we weren't going to talk about money. This isn't about the money."

"It's always going to be about the money." The muscles in his dad's neck looked like they were flexing.

"We need to set some rules," Benji's mom said.

More rules? That was the last thing they needed.

"You are to ask permission before going *anywhere*," his mom continued. "Whether it's out for pizza or off to Boston, you ask first."

"You should know to ask, Felix." Ms. Rannells tried to look at her son, but his chin was snugly against his chest and his focus was on his hands.

"There will be no more skipping school. Not one minute." Benji's mom tapped the table with her index finger as she said the last three words.

"And you will stop the excess spending," his dad said. "Immediately. A twelve-year-old boy doesn't need to spend more than ten dollars a day. Ever."

"Am I fired?" Reggie asked, looking at Benji's father.

"Jack, please." Benji's mom put a hand on her husband's. "You're getting upset."

"I *am* upset." He crossed his arms. "Why are we living in a hotel? Why are we letting our son burn through five million dollars? This should make us all upset."

"We're living in a hotel because the house is being worked on, and I need to be near Felix for a month. We're business partn—"

"You are not a business!" Benji's dad stood up quickly, and his chair fell over.

"Jack," his mom said.

"I'm sorry. This has gotten out of control." Benji's dad made a show of looking at his watch. "I'm late." He kissed his wife on the cheek and then touched Benji's shoulder briefly before leaving.

"He has a flight to San Francisco this afternoon. I'm sorry," Benji's mom said to Ms. Rannells. "This has been hard on him. On all of us."

Benji bit back a laugh. Getting five million dollars was not a burden. They didn't even know about the hard part.

"We agree to your rules," Felix said. Benji was surprised to hear him speak. "We won't run off again. We won't skip school. We'll be responsible with the money. But Reggie still works for us through the end of his contract."

Reggie took off his glasses and exchanged a look with Benji. There was no contract.

Felix, look at you telling a white lie, Benji thought.

"That's a start, but this is going to require a longer conversation," Benji's mom said.

"You're a millionaire, but I still worry." Ms. Rannells pulled Felix in and kissed his forehead. "Please try not to give me a heart attack. I'm too young."

"I won't, Mom," Felix said.

"And, Reggie," Benji's mom said, not quite done with the lecture. "I know they're your employer." She shook her head as she said the last word. "But they're also kids. Call me if you have any questions. Rides to and from school and to the movies are normal twelve-year-old trips. A lift to Boston on a school day is not. Use your head."

"I would never put my bosses in harm's way," he said.

Benji's eyes grew wide. Reggie hadn't exactly agreed with his mother. And by the look on her face, she knew it.

"Eat some breakfast," she said to Benji. "And don't be late for school."

• • •

The morning quickly improved when Felix decided to ride to school with his mom. Not that Benji didn't want Felix around. They were friends now. But with Felix and Freebie not part of the morning car pool, Benji could finally pull up to Stirling Middle School in the Bugatti.

The silver-and-black car resembled the Batmobile if Benji squinted at it. It sat low to the road and could probably slide beneath a big rig (like Benji had seen in several action movies). The controls and dashboard were black-and-gray carbon fiber except for a cherry-red start button. The leather-and-suede seats felt like a warm hug—like the car was saying "I love you, Benji."

Unfortunately, Reggie wasn't amazing at driving a stick. The car jerked and stalled all the way to school and in the drop-off line. It was the loudest vehicle among all the minivans and SUVs. Still, as he stepped out of the car, everyone took pictures. Even the teachers had their phones out. Benji smiled and posed next to the Bugatti. He knew most people would probably prefer a picture of just the car.

Mr. Palomino eventually waved Reggie away, but not before taking his own selfie in the passenger seat. Benji headed to his locker, where he was surprised to find Alma waiting for him. She sang to herself until she spotted him.

He ran his tongue over his braces. He wished he'd brushed a second time after breakfast.

"Here," she said, handing him an envelope.

"What is it?"

"A thank-you card or an I'm-sorry card." She paused and tucked a piece of hair behind her ear. "I wasn't very nice to you at my house. I mean . . . You offered to take me to Disney World and I . . . I was judgey."

"It's fine," he said.

"No." She shook her head. "I should have been nicer."

"You should have said yes," he joked.

She shrugged. "Maybe next time."

Benji did not know how to reply. The floor of the hallway looked wavy. The rows of lockers closed in. The lights got brighter.

"You okay?" she asked.

The bell rang before he could answer.

"See ya at lunch." She smiled and left.

Benji still couldn't understand what was happening. He

looked at the envelope in his hands. The sweat from his palms made the ink in his name smear. He grabbed it by the corner and blew on the writing to preserve its perfection.

"You're late," a teacher reminded him from her doorway. "Homeroom has begun."

"Sorry." He gently placed the envelope inside his science notebook and rushed into the classroom. As Ms. Chenoweth took attendance, he used the cap of a pen to open the envelope carefully. He didn't want to damage anything.

On the front of the card was *Thank you,* handwritten in scrolly letters surrounded by flowers and hearts (hearts!). Sure, hearts were an ordinary doodle and easier to draw than even stars. He tried not to let his own heart burst. On the inside was a short note.

Dear Benji,
Thank you for inviting me to Disney. I'm sorry I couldn't go. (And sorry I acted that way.) You're a nice guy.
Your friend,
Alma

He read it again and again until someone tore it out of his hand.

"Hey!" he yelled.

"What's this?" Aidan waved the card around. "A love note?"

"No." Benji shoved back his chair and stood up. He was taller than Aidan—he was taller than everyone. But they all knew he was more of a teddy bear than a grizzly.

Aidan read the note. "Ohhh. It's from Alma." He used the card to fan his face.

"Can I have that back?"

"Sure, Barney." Aidan held out the card and dropped it just as Benji reached for it. The perfect card fluttered to the ground, and Aidan "accidentally" stepped on it as he walked out.

Benji scooped it up. The front had an imprint of Aidan's sneaker. Benji felt like he wanted to hit something—or even someone.

Chapter $21

WEDNESDAY, NOVEMBER 10

Felix

Felix dribbled across the baseline, stopped just below the basket, and shot a fadeaway.

Swish!

"Ugh!" Benji replied.

"You've got this," Felix said.

They'd rented the gym at the Freemont Country Club for two hours after school. They decided playing one-on-one wasn't fair—Benji was huge, and Felix was fast. So they played Horse. But instead of spelling out *horse*, they spelled out *money*, and Benji already had *M, O, N,* and *E*. While Felix had only an *M*.

Benji took his turn and missed. Freebie chased down the rebound.

"Rematch?" Benji asked.

"We'll play again after we spend a hundred thousand dollars," Felix said. "That was the deal."

Spending money felt like a constant job. Felix would rather play basketball and video games, but there were dollars to burn. For every round of Money they played, they agreed to take a break and spend *money*.

"I should probably give up basketball. You've already shattered my confidence," Benji said, and Felix worried he might not be joking.

They sat on the bench and each opened a laptop. Underneath them, Freebie tried to chew through a basketball.

"What should we buy now?" Benji asked. "Another drone?"

"We've already bought three," Felix said. "They're still in the boxes." The deliveries from Monday's online shopping spree were flooding the hotel.

"Then let's buy clothes," Benji suggested. "You definitely need new clothes."

"What's wrong with my clothes?" Felix wasn't sure why he was getting defensive.

"They don't cost millions." Benji shook his head. "You like jeans, right?"

"Yeah." It was all Felix wore except when playing basketball.

Benji tapped away on the keyboard. "Let's see. World's most expensive jeans?" He kept his eyes on the screen.

"Well?" Felix asked, petting Freebie.

"I found some at Neiman Marcus for four thousand dollars," Benji said. "Wait! Wait! Check this out. It's a site for movie memorabilia!" Benji turned his screen for Felix to see. "We can buy clothes that were worn by actors in movies!"

Felix nodded but didn't share Benji's excitement.

"We can buy a Stormtrooper costume for fifteen thousand dollars." Benji dramatically pressed a button on his keyboard. "There! We just did. I wish Halloween wasn't over." He smiled. "What's your favorite movie?"

"I don't know." Honestly, he didn't have a *favorite* favorite.

"Do you like *Lord of the Rings*?"

"Yeah."

"Good. Because you now own Frodo's pants for nine thousand dollars."

"Lucky me."

"And I'm getting the robe worn by Obi-Wan." Benji danced in his seat but suddenly stopped. "Ew, it's from *Phantom Menace*. That's a waste of twenty grand."

"To us, there's no such thing as waste," Felix reminded him. He tried not to think what $20,000 would mean to his mom or Georgie.

"I really want a leather jacket worn in one of the Terminator movies," Benji sighed. "But I can't find one."

"Your life is so hard," Felix joked.

"Do you want me to stop?" Benji yanked his hands off the keyboard like a thief caught stealing.

"No. You're doing great."

"Yeah. I'm not good at a lot of things—like lay-ups, free throws, jump shots—but I can waste money." Benji cracked his knuckles and got back to work.

"We've still got millions to spend, Benji," Felix said. "There's no way—"

"No. No. No!" Benji jumped up, knocking his laptop to the floor, and covered Felix's mouth with his giant hand, which smelled like basketball leather. "No negativity. Be positive, buddy. We haven't even looked at footwear yet!"

Felix nodded, and Benji released him. Felix expected Benji to buy something like slippers worn by Daniel Radcliffe in a Harry Potter movie. Nope, Benji filled his cart with vintage Air Jordans. He had $172,005 worth of sneakers in his online cart, ready to pay, when they checked in with Mr. Trulz. He said, "Only shoes in your sizes." So Benji was limited to size 10 Jeters, Kobes, Transformers, and Blackouts for $77,010. Nothing was available in a size 6 for Felix, but he wasn't disappointed, because he loved his Air Flights. He bought a sneaker-cleaning kit instead.

"Impressive. Let's play one more game before I gotta go." Felix grabbed a basketball from the rack. "I'm helping Georgie and Michelle with wedding stuff."

"What kind of wedding stuff?"

"I don't know. Maybe I can pick the cake or something.

They feel like they need to include me in the plans because we're paying for it."

"Cake tasting sounds like something I'd be good at. Can I come?" Benji set aside his laptop.

"Sure."

"And I'm only playing ball if you spot me a few letters. You have *M, O,* and *N.*"

"No. Just an *M* and *O,*" Felix replied.

"Fine. I go first."

Benji dribbled to the free-throw line and sank a shot. A rare occurrence, if Felix was honest.

"That was lucky," Benji admitted.

Felix took a ball and shot from the free-throw line. It skimmed the rim and missed.

"And now you have an *N.*" Benji dribbled beyond the three-point arc. "I've been playing basketball since I was four. My dad signed me up to play with the kids already in kindergarten and first grade. Everyone thought I was going to be a star. I was a foot taller than the others, and we used a six-foot-high basket. I could practically dunk." He shot the ball, and it bounced off the backboard.

Felix grabbed the rebound. "You could dunk?"

"I said *practically.* Everyone—especially my parents—thought I was going to be great, and now I might not make the middle school team. My basketball career is over before it started."

Felix didn't know how to reply. Benji wasn't the best player, but he was big, and that had to count for something. Felix made a simple right-handed lay-up and passed the ball to Benji.

"It's just the one thing I really want. Ya know?" Benji took his ball and made the lay-up. "It would definitely make my parents happy. My dad is ready to rearrange his travel schedule to be at the games. If I have to tell him I'm not on the team . . . that'll suck."

Benji shot the ball.

And missed.

"I'm sure you'll make the team," Felix said. It was just words. Words that he hoped would make Benji feel better and would also change the subject.

FIRST BANK OF NEW YORK

Current Balance: $3,743,858.59

RECENT TRANSACTIONS

Nov 10, Sneaker Head Warehouse	−$77,010.00
Nov 10, FromTheMovies.com	−$44,000.00
Nov 10, Freemont Country Club (Gymnasium Rental)	
	−$800.00
Nov 10, Downtown Donuts	−$1,275.00

Chapter $22

THURSDAY, NOVEMBER 11

Benji

As required, Benji got permission before leaving the hotel and spending Veterans Day in New York City. It was easy because Ms. Rannells, Georgie, and Reggie were all chaperoning.

"It's one of the most expensive cities in the world," Benji had said to Felix—not his parents. "We can do some real damage."

To the parents, he had said, "It's Veterans Day, and we want to go to New York to visit museums and stuff."

Reggie drove them to the Metro-North station, and from there they took the ninety-minute train ride into the city.

"Where are we going first?" Felix asked when they arrived at Grand Central.

"Comic book store. It's not far." Benji adjusted his vintage Hermès bag on his shoulder. He'd stuffed it with bags of M&M's and barbecue potato chips. Left empty, it sagged in the middle and just didn't look right. Plus, snacks!—always a good idea.

"I've got an appointment to try on wedding gowns," Georgie said. It was her sole reason for taking a day off work.

They split up. Ms. Rannells and Georgie headed off to a morning of fancy dresses, and the guys went to explore the world's best literature.

Benji didn't like regular books. The words on *those* pages twisted and seemed to move in front of his eyes. If he really focused, he could read about two sentences well, but by the time he got to the third or fourth, he'd have forgotten the first. Comics and graphic novels were different. The stories stuck. The words didn't get messed up in his brain.

Using the map on his phone, Benji led them to the store. He pulled open the door, ran up the narrow stairs, and took a deep breath. It smelled of paper and ink and awesome.

"Excuse me," Benji said to the green-haired girl behind the counter. "Do you have *Action Comics* number one? It's basically Superman's first comic." He'd seen a YouTube video that said someone had spent three million dollars for a mint edition.

"I know, and no. We don't have it." She drummed her black fingernails on the glass counter.

"Look at that one." Felix pointed to the rack behind the

counter. They had an *X-Men* for $1,200. But Benji had a suspicion that these were not their best books. They probably kept the good stuff in the back.

"What are your oldest comics? I want to buy them." He leaned on the counter.

"We have a *Batman* issue one. But you can't afford it."

"How much?" Benji knew he must look like a normal kid—well, a charming kid—coming into the store with maybe twenty dollars in his pocket. Next time, he should wear a suit so people would take him seriously.

"How much do you think?"

"A million dollars," he answered, knowing it was really wishful thinking.

"Bingo," the clerk said with no enthusiasm. She held out her palm and put her other hand on her hip.

"I'll take three." In a smooth move—he'd had plenty of practice—Benji whipped out his debit card and slapped it into her hand.

She didn't move other than to raise an eyebrow. "We have one, and it's forty-one thousand dollars."

"Then I'll take just one."

"We also want that *X-Men*, a *Captain America,* and *The Walking Dead,*" Felix added.

"Ring 'em up!" Benji pointed to the debit card still in her hand. Then he added, "We're Laura Friendly's millionaire boys." That usually worked in the Albany area. Hopefully, their fame extended to the city.

"I need to call my boss," the girl said.

"No worries." Benji smiled. "We'll look around while we wait."

They found Reggie flipping through some historical graphic novels.

"These are about the Spanish Inquisition. Brilliant work. You should check them out." One cover was a mixture of fire and demons and men in robes. It didn't look too bad.

"Sure," Benji said. He grabbed a mesh basket by the door and threw in a Spanish Inquisition comic.

Then he went around the store and grabbed anything that looked interesting—which wasn't hard in a comic book store. His basket weighed five pounds in no time.

"Excuse me," the girl behind the counter called. She held a phone to her ear. "Were you interested in other rare comics besides *Batman*?"

"Yes," Felix answered before Benji.

In the end, they bought $68,980 in comic books—most of which they had shipped to the hotel. They shoved the five most expensive ones into Benji's Hermès handbag.

"Let's get lunch," Benji suggested. "We *should* go to the fanciest restaurant in New York, where they serve thousand-dollar fish eggs." He wrinkled his nose. "But I really want a burger."

They found a restaurant, and after they ordered cheeseburgers (and one bean burger for Reggie), fries, and milk shakes, they pulled out the comics.

Benji slowly peeled back the plastic case. The waiter noticed and nearly lost his mind.

"Is that real? A *Batman* number one? You can't open that. It'll lose all its value." He looked ready to tear it out of Benji's hands. A few customers turned and looked at them.

"It's mine" was all Benji could think to say.

"It's literature," Reggie added, stroking his dark beard. "It's meant to be read and enjoyed. If Aristotle was here, he'd say everything has a *telos*—a purpose or what it's meant to be. This comic book *telos* is not to reside under a plastic jail. This object has lost its purpose, and this boy will reestablish the intent, restoring order to the world."

"What?" the waiter yelled.

"I'm confused too," Benji said with a shrug. "He does this a lot. Mini-philosophy lectures that make no sense." He almost felt bad for the waiter.

"It's art. You can't open it!" the waiter insisted.

"It's definitely not art," Benji said. "We're not allowed art."

"You can't open it," the waiter said again with hands clenched into fists.

"Yes, I can." Benji slid the comic book out, and the waiter actually screamed. The manager had to come over, and they were given a new server who didn't care about the cash value or *telos* of a comic book.

Felix and Benji read the *Batman* at the same time, both leaning over it. When the food came, Felix accidentally dropped a small blob of ketchup on one page. He froze as if waiting for someone to yell—maybe the waiter again. But Benji just turned the page with his greasy fingers.

They read all the comics and didn't worry about dripping milk shake on them or bending the covers. On the way out, they threw away the plastic that had kept the pages safe for years. The comics had ended up in the wrong hands.

Or, they had ended up in the perfect hands.

Chapter $23

THURSDAY, NOVEMBER 11

Felix

Going to a bridal shop was not at the top of Felix's to-do list, but Georgie had called and asked him to drop in.

"I'm not going dress shopping." Benji refused to step into the store. "If you need someone to sample cakes, I'm your man."

"You're carrying an Hermès purse," Felix reminded him.

"True." Benji nodded. "But I didn't have to go to a store to buy it." He stayed outside and sat on a bench.

A saleslady escorted Felix into the back of the shop. He found Georgie standing on a platform in front of a three-panel mirror.

"Wow," Felix said. "You look pretty, Georgie."

She stopped fiddling with the headpiece and turned to him. "Isn't it the perfect dress?"

He nodded.

"And it hardly needs any alterations, which is good. We don't have much time." She smoothed the fabric across her stomach.

"Good." He didn't know anything about alterations or how long they might take. His mom had hemmed his pants before. They were always at least an inch too long. She was able to do it in one night while watching *Dateline*.

"It costs a little over six thousand dollars," Georgie continued. "But I think it's worth it. I never imagined I could wear a *Limor Rosen*."

He jerked back slightly. He'd spent more than that on Frodo's pants, but six thousand dollars was a fortune to Georgie and Michelle—and *had* been to him, last month.

"That's too much money, Georgie," his mother said. Felix turned to see her sitting in a high-back maroon chair and sipping a cup of tea.

"I know." Georgie made a pouty face. "What do you think, Felix?"

"Do not ask your brother to buy your gown. He's done enough. And I'd like to buy your dress, but I don't have six thousand dollars to spend. We'll need to find something reasonable." His mom set down her fancy teacup.

"Mom, I really want this dress." Georgie clasped her hands. "Felix has money. It's not that much, considering."

"No." His mom stood up and looked Felix in the eyes. "Wait outside."

"Moooooom," Georgie whined, and she sounded six, not twenty.

Felix felt relieved that he didn't have to tell Georgie no. If she knew he'd just spent thousands on comics but couldn't buy her a gown, she'd never understand.

"What's wrong?" Benji asked when Felix stepped outside.

"Nothing."

"Something," Benji said. "I can tell because you chew your thumbnail when you're stressed."

Felix pulled his hand from his mouth. "Do not. And nothing is wrong."

"Liar." Benji leaned back on the bench. "What are we doing next? We should rent a helicopter to fly us over the city."

"I hate this game!" Felix snapped.

Both Reggie and Benji looked up at him.

"What game?" Reggie asked.

"I Spy," Benji answered quickly. "I beg him to play, but he won't."

Benji got up from the bench and draped an arm over Felix's shoulder. "What do you want to play, buddy?" He walked them a few steps from Reggie.

"I knew something was wrong," Benji continued. "Why are you freaking out?"

"I hate that we can't buy stuff for other people. It's not fair. It's not right. What's the point of all the money if we

can't share it? It's not like I just want to give it to strangers."
And just then, Felix looked up and saw, down the street,
a homeless woman with a dog begging for change with a
paper coffee cup, and he felt even worse.

"Once we win, you can do whatever you want with the
money," Benji reminded him.

"But that's after the wedding, and Georgie won't need a
wedding dress in December. She wants one now."

"Oh," Benji said.

"I just want to buy a wedding dress," Felix whined. He
realized he sounded like Georgie.

Suddenly, Benji slapped him in the chest. "You totally can!"

"No." Felix pushed Benji away. He didn't seem to be listening at all. "We can't buy stuff for other people. A wedding dress is definitely stuff."

"No." Benji crossed his arms. "You said, 'I just want to
buy a wedding dress.' And you can. For yourself."

Felix shook his head instinctively, but as he thought
about it, he realized Benji was right. "I can buy the dress for
me! I just have to wear it once. That's what the rules say. I
have to use what I buy. Then Georgie can *borrow* it."

"I'll buy a wedding dress too," Benji said. "Because
they're more expensive than most guys' clothes, right?"

Felix turned to go back into the store just as Georgie
and his mom came out. Georgie's eyes were red.

"We'll find something as beautiful as you are," his mom said as she rubbed Georgie's back.

"Georgie! Georgie!" Felix jumped in front of his sister. "I'm going to buy your dress." Then he looked at Benji, who'd been the genius behind the idea. "*We're* going to buy your dress."

His mom tilted her head. "Felix, I told you—"

"Come on. Let's do this." Benji pulled open the door to the shop, no longer put off by dress shopping. "Time to get fancy."

Georgie didn't hesitate. She hurried back into the store. Felix tried to follow, but his mom grabbed his arm.

"Why are you doing this?" she asked, and now it was her eyes that looked red. "I told you I wanted to buy her dress. It means something to me."

"But you can't afford it." The words escaped his mouth before he could consider their impact.

"I can't afford *that* dress, but we could have found a different one."

"But Georgie really wants this dress."

She gave him a challenging look. "And I really wanted to be the one who bought it for her."

He wished he could just slide six thousand dollars into his mom's wallet. Then she could buy the dress and everyone would be happy.

"Wait, you can buy the dress," Felix said, remembering

the money he'd won at the Celtics game. "Use the ten thousand I gave you."

"No. Absolutely not." She sighed. "You're not listening to me, Felix. It's not just about the price tag. Something doesn't have to be expensive to be special. You should know that." She shook her head, and maybe for the first time in his life, he could feel she was disappointed in him.

She joined Reggie on the bench.

"I'm sorry," Felix said.

She just waved away his apology like it was an annoying fly. He hadn't meant to make his mom feel bad or to keep her from buying Georgie a wedding gown. Did it matter who actually paid for it if Georgie was happy? His mom was selfish for demanding that Georgie buy something in her price range. Felix was the good guy in this situation.

He looked back at his mom. Her head was in her hands. Good guys didn't make other people cry on public benches. If he knew what to say or how to fix his mistake, he'd go over to her. But he was clueless, so he went inside to buy a gown.

FIRST BANK OF NEW YORK

Current Balance: $3,653,191.77

RECENT TRANSACTIONS

Nov 11, Sarah's Bridal Boutique   -$17,248.68

Nov 11, Side of Fries Restaurant   -$119.23

Nov 11, Central NY Comics   -$68,980.00

Nov 11, MTA (Round-Trip Passenger Tickets)   -$257.50

Chapter $24

Benji

The next morning, Reggie drove Benji and Felix to school in the Porsche. Felix sat in the back and stroked Freebie's head. Benji had already asked him three times if he was okay, and Felix had insisted—three times—that he was fine. Since they'd bought the wedding gowns, Felix had been acting weird, and Benji knew it wasn't because they now owned frilly dresses.

When they got to school, Felix shuffled inside and didn't respond to anyone's hellos. Benji talked to everyone. He would have signed autographs and posed for pictures if anyone had asked. Then he walked by the doughnut stand to check on everything and ran into Aidan and Luke.

"Hey, any jelly left?" Benji asked. He'd already had breakfast at the hotel, but he could make room for a doughnut.

"Benji, are we having pizza for lunch today?" Aidan ignored Benji's question and asked his own.

"Of course." Benji held up his hand, expecting a high five for his generosity.

Instead, Aidan groaned. "Could we get something else?"

"All we do is eat pizza," Luke added, and grabbed his stomach like it caused him pain.

"What do you want?" Benji asked.

"Tacos," they answered in unison, and it didn't sound spontaneous.

"Tacos?" Benji repeated.

"Yeah, tacos," Aidan said. "Everyone is complaining about the pizza."

Why would they complain about pizza? Pizza is the best.

"I like tacos," Benji said. "I'll see what I can do."

"Thanks." Aidan clapped him on the back and walked off with Luke. Benji heard him say to Luke, "I told you he'd do it."

Benji didn't understand what had just happened. He didn't mind buying tacos or sandwiches or chicken nuggets. He could afford all of it. But what did his "friends" expect from him?

"Are you okay?" Suddenly Alma was standing in front of him.

"Yeah."

"You've been standing in the same spot for two minutes," she said.

He shook his head and realized she was right.

"Can I ask you a question? Do you like tacos?"

"I like tacos." She smiled, and his heart sped up.

"Good. I'm buying tacos for lunch. You can have some." Maybe Aidan and Luke's idea wasn't bad.

"No, thank you."

"Why not?" He fought to keep his voice level. All girls were a bit of a mystery, but Alma took it to the next level. "I want to do something nice for you. That's all. Why can't I buy you lunch?"

"You're buying the whole school lunch." She gestured to the crowded hallway. "That's not for me."

"I can order something special for you. Something no one else gets. Anything you want." He flashed his biggest smile and hoped he didn't have any breakfast left in his braces.

"That's not necessary," she said. "I brought my lunch. And you don't need to buy me anything."

"Why won't you let me do something nice for you?"

"You want to do something nice?" she asked. "You can help me hang these posters." She held out a small stack of homemade signs.

DRAMA CLUB FUNDRAISER
FOOD, VENDORS, AUCTION, ENTERTAINMENT
DECEMBER 1ST
6PM–8PM

"Hey," he said, cheering up. "It's on December first."

"Just like you requested. You still offering to supply pizza or other food?" She straightened her purple cat ears. "It's not for me. It's for the drama club."

"Absolutely. And I'll help you hang them up." He took the stack. "Posters today, maybe I can buy you lunch tomorrow . . . or, um, on Monday."

"Benji, if you keep buying people food and offering trips to Disney, they'll want to hang out with you. But then how will you know who your real friends are?" She walked off, not giving him a chance to reply. Not that he'd know what to say.

• • •

After open gym, it was officially the weekend and time for spending serious money. But first, they had to wear the wedding dresses or the troll would shut down the challenge.

"Come on," Benji begged. He stood in the living room of Felix's suite, waiting for his partner.

The bedroom door opened slowly like in a horror movie. But instead of a monster, there was Felix in Georgie's dream wedding gown. It fit him horribly. The shoulder straps fell down to his elbows, and the skirt bunched at his feet.

Benji laughed. "You look like a cream puff."

"And you look like a frozen fish," Felix said.

"You're right. A mermaid cut is not flattering on a guy my size." He exaggerated a frown.

"A *what* cut?"

"Mermaid. That's what the saleslady called it." Benji held his head up high, proud to know something Felix didn't.

"I hate this dress, and not just because I have to wear it," Felix mumbled. "Now what?"

"Selfies. To send to the troll." Benji held up his phone and took a few pictures. "Then we'll go order something at the restaurant, so we can say we wore the dresses out."

"Let's do it." Felix attached Freebie's leash, and they headed to the elevator.

The restaurant was empty except for a few employees. Benji and Felix sat at the bar and ordered sodas.

"Special occasion?" the bartender asked. "Want your root beer in a champagne flute?"

"Ha ha," Benji replied.

The bartender gave them their drinks in regular glasses. Two boys had never drunk sodas so fast. They were about to leave when Benji noticed a picture of Laura Friendly on the television.

"Can you turn that up?" he asked.

When the sound came on, it wasn't Laura Friendly on the screen anymore. It was a country singer named Danny Devon yelling at the camera.

"That BLEEEP Laura Friendly and the BLEEEEP

maggots that work at Friendly Connect are BLEEEEP your privacy and selling your BLEEEEP soul to the highest BLEEEEP bidder. They'd BLEEEEEP do anything to make a dollar. Our entire society is a BLEEEEP mess because of BLEEEP people like Laura Friendly and BLEEEEEP her BLEEEEP BLEEEP BLEEEEP."

Felix, Benji, and the bartender all stared at the television.

"I don't even know what he's saying at the end because there's so much being bleeped out." Benji curled his lip.

"He's trashing Laura Friendly," Felix said.

"Yeah, he is."

"And she's our friend!"

"She is?"

"Yes! We need to do something." Felix turned to Benji and looked completely serious.

"What do you suggest?"

"I don't know." Felix pushed away his empty soda glass, and the bartender refilled it. "Ms. Friendly is nice."

"Is she?"

"She gave us five million dollars," Felix said.

Benji whispered, "No, she gave us a challenge to spend over five million dollars. If she'd given us five million dollars, I'd call her nice."

"Whatever. I don't like this guy attacking Ms. Friendly. We need to do something. Think, Benji. You're the creative one."

I am? Artists, musicians, and writers were creative. Benji was none of those things.

"I guess we can prank him," Benji suggested.

"Yes! And we have millions of dollars at our disposal. How do we get revenge?" Felix asked. He pounded his left fist in his right palm.

Benji liked this idea. Getting revenge with a nearly unlimited budget opened up the possibilities. Filling Danny Devon's pool with Jell-O (assuming the singer had a pool), feeding pigeons near his sports car (assuming he had a sports car), or making a mock video of his hit song starring cats.

"Well?" Felix asked.

"Hang on." A good idea sprouted in Benji's brain, along with the ridiculous ideas. He Googled Danny Devon's appearances on his phone.

"He has a concert. Tomorrow night. In Chicago!" Benji said. "We buy tickets. All the available tickets for his show."

"How is that a prank?" Felix tilted his head and stared.

"When Danny Devon comes out onstage, he'll be singing to empty seats. To nobody!" Benji rubbed his fingernails on his shirt and then blew on them.

"But we have to use what we buy," Felix said.

"We can go to the concert. And if the troll insists, we'll even sit in every seat. For at least a few seconds."

Felix leaned closer to Benji to look at the phone screen. "How many tickets are there?"

"The Chicago Theatre isn't huge, not like a stadium." Benji pointed to the screen. "Says it only seats four thousand. And . . ." Benji clicked the available tickets button. "There are over a thousand tickets available right now."

Felix squished his eyebrows together. "Sounds like he's already playing to a quarter-empty theater."

"No, people buy the tickets last minute at half price, or for even less, and the show would technically *sell out*." His parents had bought tickets this way before in New York.

"Okay." Felix nodded. "Buy them all."

Using their money for revenge, this was new. This was awesome. This was creative.

Chapter $25

Felix

That morning, the T. rex and triceratops skulls arrived at the Grand Regency. The boys suspected their parents would not be enthusiastic about their paleontology purchases. So they asked Reggie if they could "hide" the fossils in his suite.

"Why don't you just get a storage space?" Reggie replied.

But Benji came up with a better idea. "We'll rent more rooms."

So the T. rex, which they named Banana Teeth, and Trip, the triceratops, each got their own room on the seventh floor. The boys also stored their shoe collection, their one handbag, and their various "toys" in 704 and 705. Then they wasted the rest of their Saturday afternoon filling up virtual shopping carts with more stuff (giant pool floats, VR headsets, new gaming systems, extra laptops and iPads) before it was finally time to head to the Danny Devon concert.

Felix's mom gave him permission to go to the show. Maybe she said yes because she already had plans with Georgie and Michelle. Or maybe because he didn't mention that the concert was in Chicago. He'd just said, "Reggie's driving," which was partly true. He drove them to the airport. Felix was becoming an expert at rule-bending.

When they told Reggie their Saturday night plans, Reggie did a cartwheel—literally, in the middle of the hotel lobby. Turned out, he was a big Danny Devon fan and even offered to buy his own ticket. That wasn't happening.

"Why do you like DD? Does he sing about philosophy or something?" Benji asked on the plane. They had, of course, booked private transportation.

"Not exactly. Though a lot of songs can be tied back to philosophy, especially value theory and the essential meaning of life."

"Stop." Benji held up a hand. "You're going to make me hate all music."

"I already hate Danny Devon," Felix said. "He's a jerk."

"Have I told you about the philosopher David Hume?" Reggie asked, but didn't wait for an answer. "He has a quote, 'The life of man is of no greater importance to the universe than that of an oyster.' Think about that for a minute."

"That doesn't make any sense," Benji said instantly—not even bothering to think about it for five seconds.

Reggie clasped his hands and looked at Felix. "You're wasting your limited time and energy hating Danny Devon. It is not impacting Danny Devon in the slightest. You're only harming *your* soul and *your* happiness."

"He'll be impacted in a few hours." Benji pulled up the hood on his Obi-Wan robe, tapped his fingertips together, and added an evil laugh.

"Consider this," Reggie said. "Would you call an oyster a jerk? Is an oyster worth your scorn?"

Felix shrugged. "I don't talk to many oysters."

"Exactly!" Reggie leaned back and smiled.

When they got to the concert, scanning the tickets took over an hour because they had to swipe through 1,442 of them. (The rules clearly stated they had to use what they bought, and Mr. Trulz agreed that scanning the tickets counted as "using.") In just one day, they'd bought a quarter of all the seats in the theater.

"Gee, where should we sit?" Benji asked when they got inside. He held out his arm and spun around. The tail of his brown robe flared behind him.

"Should we go to the back?" Felix asked. "So it'll seem emptier. But I want to be close enough to see his face."

"I'll be in the front row." Reggie left, not waiting for their decision and the boys reluctantly followed.

Thanks to their mass ticket-buying, the first ten rows of the venue were mostly empty. Some people tried to sneak into the section, but security kept them out.

After an opening act, the lights dimmed and fog rolled across the audience. The band did not step out on the stage but rose from some hidden basement. Then a song began that made Felix's eardrums pulse.

Danny Devon—the foulmouthed Laura Friendly hater—danced, jumped, and ran across the stage. There were still plenty of fans screaming and jumping.

"I don't think he cares!" Felix yelled into Benji's ear.

Reggie sang along and danced on his seat. He clearly didn't consider Danny Devon an oyster.

The first song seemed to last twenty minutes. When it finally ended, a pressure released inside Felix's head.

Danny Devon stepped to the front edge of the stage. He held out his arms and threw his head back to take in all the cheering. His chest rose with each deep breath. Then he opened his eyes and looked at the front row.

"What the BLEEP is this?"

(Felix had to insert his own bleep.)

Benji held up his cell phone and recorded the scene.

"Where are all your fans? Loser!" Benji yelled.

"Why are you such a jerk?" Felix screamed.

Reggie jumped down from his chair and said to Felix and Benji, "I'll just find another seat." Then he flashed Danny Devon a quick thumbs-up.

"Is this a joke?" Danny Devon glanced back at his band. A guitarist just shrugged.

"You owe Laura Friendly an apology," Felix said, though he knew there was no way that was happening.

Benji kept his phone aimed at the stage in case the singer decided to oblige.

"Forget you. Forget her," Danny Devon said, and added a hand gesture worthy of another bleep.

"All these empty seats, we bought them," Benji said, and waved toward the empty spots. "And we can keep buying seats until you apologize."

"Doesn't matter who buys the seats. I still get paid." The singer swore again and started the next song. The music seemed louder and more aggressive, even though it was a song about kissing in the back of a pickup truck.

Is he trying to hurt us with sound waves? Felix wondered.

Benji screamed something in Felix's ear, but he couldn't hear. So Benji texted.

BENJI: Let's get out of here

FELIX: OK

They texted Reggie, too, but he wanted to stay.

"I think we got what we wanted," Benji said as they stood in line at the concession stand.

"Did we?" Felix asked. "We got revenge by paying him to do something he was going to do if we were here or not."

"Trust me. The empty seats got to him. He wasn't happy," Benji said. "But you don't seem happy either."

"I'm just tired," Felix said. "Spending this money is

exhausting, and we've got a long way to go." He'd looked at the banking app less than an hour ago. Even with the concert tickets, the private jet, and eight hours wasted online shopping, they weren't even halfway.

"Don't worry, buddy. We'll spend the money. All of it." Benji stood up straighter and dramatically put up his hood. "The Force is with us, young Skywalker. Believe in the Force."

Felix rolled his eyes. "You look ridiculous in that."

"But it's very comfortable. I like to wear it after I get out of the shower."

"Too much information."

They got to the front of the line, and Benji ordered popcorn, nuts, eight different candies, and soda. They wouldn't be able to eat all the snacks. Throwing away a big portion of their food had become standard, and the guilt stung every time.

They found seats near a window.

"A few weeks ago, I'd never imagined I'd spend a Saturday night in Chicago," Felix said as he opened a box of Milk Duds.

"Me either. I usually spend weekends hanging out with friends. Playing video games or watching movies. What about you?"

"Same." And by that, he meant sitting in his apartment. Alone.

"When we move out of the hotel, you need to come over to my house," Benji said. "I'm going to need to see Freebie."

"Yeah." *What will happen to Freebie if we don't win?* Felix refused to consider it. "What are you going to do with your millions—the real millions—when we win?"

"I don't know. Buy a car?" Benji shoveled a handful of popcorn into his mouth. "You?"

"I'll give some money to my mom to pay bills and stuff, and so she can go back to school." Felix sipped his soda. "After that, I'm going into real estate. I'm buying my mom a house. I'm buying Georgie and Michelle a house. I'm buying everyone a house."

"What about your dad?" Benji asked.

"My dad?" Felix's head snapped in Benji's direction. "What about him?"

"Nothing. You never mentioned him. But I assume you have one or had one. That's what we were taught in fifth-grade family life class. When they separated the girls into one room and the boys into the other, and they explained the changes—"

"I remember," Felix said. "I haven't seen my dad in years. He's not part of my life."

"Oh." Benji shrugged.

"When we first got the money," Felix continued, "and we were on the news, I worried that he might just show up and ask for a million dollars. 'Hey, son, I love you and thought you might be able to give your old pops a few million.'" Felix did his best dad imitation, but he honestly didn't think he'd recognize his father's voice.

"I even imagined slamming the door in his face," Felix continued. "I tried to think of a clever comeback like 'I'm sorry. Have we met?'"

"Did he ever show up?" Benji asked.

"No. Which is worse. Isn't it? I know if he came here right now, he'd only want money. But he didn't come for the money." Felix turned the Milk Duds box in his hand. "He doesn't want to see me, even for a million bucks."

"He must be the stupidest guy in the world." Benji put an arm around Felix's shoulders. "Forget the million dollars. He's missing out on something more important."

Felix rolled his eyes, expecting Benji to reply like an adult. *He's missing out on one great kid.*

"He's never going to meet your friends," Benji said. "And you have cool friends."

"Meaning you?"

"Yep." Benji sat up straight and lifted his chin.

"His loss."

FIRST BANK OF NEW YORK

Current Balance: $3,342,261.77

RECENT TRANSACTIONS

Nov 13, Chicago Theatre Concessions   −$53.00

Nov 13, Direct Connect Private Jets   −$45,000.00

Nov 13, The Grand Regency (Standard Rooms−18 Days)
−$8,101.31

Nov 12, TicketGrabber.com (Danny Devon Concert)
−$163,548.00

Chapter $26

SUNDAY, NOVEMBER 14

Benji

Felix insisted they devote their Sunday to spending, and he insisted they start at 8:00 a.m. Benji insisted on the backseat of the Range Rover so he could sleep an extra hour as they drove to Saratoga to buy racehorses.

Thoroughbreds cost way more than stray dogs. They purchased Leading Lady and New York Speed Machine for a total of $115,000, plus $330 per day for food and housing—or "boarding," as the horse people called it. Then they "rode" the horses once around a small warm-up track. The trainers never let go of the leashes—or "leads," as the horse people called them.

Next, they headed to see an ad guy. Sure, it was a weekend, but the ad man offered to come in when they told him how many billboards they wanted to rent.

They didn't have anything to advertise, so they put up some of Reggie's favorite philosophy quotes.

The two enemies of human happiness are pain and boredom.—Schopenhauer

All our knowledge begins with the senses, proceeds then to the understanding, and ends with reason. There is nothing higher than reason.—Kant

The life of man is of no greater importance to the universe than that of an oyster.—David Hume

Benji wanted to use his favorite philosophy quote too.

With great power comes great responsibility.—Uncle Ben

And Felix wanted to have a sign for his sister.

Congratulations, Georgie and Michelle!

In all, Benji and Felix bought two hundred digital billboards across New York at an average price of $415 per week, each. It had been a productive morning, and it was time for lunch.

"What are we going to give Georgie and Michelle for their wedding?" Benji asked as they stood at the counter in Wendy's. It wasn't going to be an expensive meal—even if they upsized everything. They just craved fast food.

"We can't buy them anything. Not even a toaster."

"I have an idea," Benji said. He'd thought of it last night while they were flying home from the Danny Devon concert. "We hire a band. A famous one, like Queen or the Beatles, but still alive."

"I guess. But we should ask Georgie first," Felix said.

"No, it's a surprise. An expensive surprise." Benji leaned closer to Felix. "Maybe a million-dollar surprise."

Felix's eyes lit up.

"So who's Georgie's favorite band? Or a favorite song?" Benji asked.

"She loves that song 'Never Ever Without You.' She cranks up the radio when it comes on."

"I know that song. It's by Apex-7. I'll look into it."

They stepped up to the cashier. "For here or to go?" she asked.

"To go," Benji said. The boys ordered their lunch, plus a baked potato for Reggie and a plain burger for Freebie, who was on a potty break. They moved to the side as they waited for their food, and an old guy ordered next.

"A small cheeseburger and a small coffee." He pulled a handful of change from his pocket.

"That'll be $3.19."

The man pushed the coins around in his palm. After a few seconds, he changed his order. "I think I'll just have coffee today."

The woman shrugged and tapped on the cash register screen.

"Wait," Benji said. "Your lunch is on me."

The man gave him a suspicious glare.

"You remind me of my grandpa," Benji said with a smile. "And I miss him so much." His grandfather was alive and well and looked nothing like this guy. Benji gave the cashier his debit card.

"Thank you." The man squeezed Benji's arm and almost looked ready to cry. All because of $3.19.

The next to place an order were a mom and her two little kids. The younger one took forever deciding between apple juice and chocolate milk. When she finally settled on dairy, Felix stepped forward to pick up the check.

"Thanks," the mom said.

Then they paid for the next guy, and the next family, and the next, and the next. They ate their food at the counter, telling everyone, "It's on us," between bites of fries and burgers. (Reggie and Freebie enjoyed a peaceful meal in the Range Rover.) After about the tenth purchase, the troll called questioning the spending.

"We're just having lunch with new friends," Benji replied.

"As long as you're on the premises, I'll allow it." So they stayed even after they'd finished eating, buying food for anyone who came in the door. Not because they were spending thousands, but because it was fun. Especially when Benji got to tell children to order a Frosty with their nuggets.

They'd just bought kids' meals for an entire soccer team of five-year-olds when Benji and Felix both got a text message.

LAURA FRIENDLY: Times Union Center in 1 hour

Benji looked up from his phone. "Is that an invitation? Or an order? Or a butt-dial?"

"I don't know. I'll text her back."

FELIX: Do you want us to be at the Times Union Center in 1 hour?

LAURA FRIENDLY: No. Now it's 59 minutes

LAURA FRIENDLY: Don't be late!

They headed to the car, and Felix told Reggie the plan. Benji thought about resisting. Just because Laura Friendly was an adult and a billionaire and the mastermind of their spending game, he didn't have to do what she said. But he was also curious. Very curious.

When they arrived at the arena, it looked deserted: no concert or game or circus happening today. Reggie parked the car in a lot next to the main door.

"Should I come in?" he asked.

"Yeah," Benji said. "We might need a witness for whatever this is."

Felix rolled his eyes. "We don't need a witness. But you can help with Freebie." He handed over the leash.

They walked into the arena and found Laura Friendly standing in the middle of the basketball court alone. The stands were dark and empty, but the Jumbotron was on. The score was zero–zero, and the teams were listed as Felix and Benji.

"Well, if it isn't the world's biggest country music fans," Laura Friendly yelled out to them.

"What is she up to?" Benji murmured.

Felix didn't answer. He jogged down the steps to the

court. Reggie and Freebie followed, and so did Benji, less enthusiastically.

"I heard you attended a concert last night." Laura Friendly crossed her arms.

"We didn't break any rules," Felix said.

"I'm not accusing you of cheating. I'm just curious why."

"Personally"—Reggie tapped his chest—"I'm a big fan of Danny Devon, but I assume you don't want to hear from me. I'm going to take the dog for a walk. Be back in a few." He waved at the boys and left the floor.

"I am *not* a fan of Danny Devon," Felix said.

"Didn't you see what he said about you? The guy hates you," Benji said, and Felix elbowed him. "Ow!"

Laura Friendly laughed. "A lot of people who don't know me, hate me. It's part of the job." Benji would not want that kind of job.

"So, you saw it?" Felix asked.

"A few seconds of his rant. I don't have the time to waste on outbursts like that."

"We watched it like ten times," Benji said.

"So why did you go to the trouble of attending his concert?" She tapped her chin.

Benji got the feeling she was looking for a specific answer. Like when Mrs. Ogilvy asked, "How did the poem make you feel?" She didn't want to know you felt bored. She wanted you to guess how she felt.

"He was a jerk, and you're our"—Felix paused—"friend."

Benji would have gone with *associate.*

"I see."

"Why did he say all those things about you?" Benji asked. "He seemed *mad* mad. Like you killed his dog."

"It's complicated, boys. My lawyers barely understand it. But when we started Friendly Connect fifteen years ago, it was a new platform that no one had ever seen. Brilliant, really. We had to write the rules while we wrote the code. The waters got murky quickly, and suddenly everyone was fighting over rights to content and privacy. We're still working on reorganizing and protecting our customers. It's safe to say, not everyone is happy with our past."

Felix nodded. Maybe he understood.

Benji shrugged. "Doesn't seem as bad as killing his dog."

Laura Friendly laughed. "I agree. For the record, I've never harmed an animal."

"He still shouldn't say that stuff," Felix added.

"He should definitely work on expanding his vocabulary. Regardless, I appreciate you coming to my defense. Not many people do. So I have a surprise for you."

Another five million dollars? Benji bit his tongue before that could slip out. He didn't exactly trust a Laura Friendly surprise. She suddenly pulled a whistle from her pocket and blew. Spotlights illuminated the entrance, and the sound of dribbling echoed through the building.

"I thought you'd like to play a little three versus three,

and I asked a few friends to join you." She gestured to the four men entering the court.

Not four men.

Four NBA players.

Four All-Star NBA players.

"What!" Felix screamed.

The guys jogged to the far basket, and each dunked the ball. Then they joined Benji, Felix, and Laura Friendly at center court.

"This is Christian Hamilton, Elijah Nichols, Xavier Cahill, and Caleb Autry." Laura Friendly introduced the players, though they needed no introduction.

Benji gave them each a high five and pulled out his cell phone for a series of selfies.

"Go ahead, pick your teams," Laura Friendly ordered. "Felix, you're small. You go first."

"I . . . I, um . . ." Felix seemed to forget how to talk.

"Indecision is not an admirable quality," Laura Friendly said. "I'll just make the teams." She divided up the players. "You only have an hour. Enjoy."

"Are you serious?" Benji asked. "We get to play with these guys for the next hour?"

"And I haven't even told you the best part yet." She paused dramatically and motioned for Felix and Benji to join her on the sideline. "You're paying for this. The price tag, half a million."

"Felix and me? Out of our five mil?" Benji asked, needing to clarify. Felix might have thought Laura Friendly was a nice person; Benji was still undecided.

"Yes. The bill is all yours. I'll call Leonard right now and tell him to pay for it. Sound good?"

"Yes!" Benji answered. Maybe Laura Friendly wasn't a monster after all.

"Are we playing or what?" Xavier Cahill asked from the court.

"Oh, we're playing." Benji pulled off his hoodie. "After we take a few more pictures."

FIRST BANK OF NEW YORK

Current Balance: $2,467,394.50

RECENT TRANSACTIONS

Nov 14, Special Services (Basketball at Times Union Center)   -$500,000.00

Nov 14, Wendy's   -$1,133.48

Nov 14, Northeast Advertising   -$249,000.00

Nov 14, Barnyard Stables (Horse Boarding) -$5,940.00

Chapter $27

MONDAY, NOVEMBER 15

Felix

Immediately after school, basketball tryouts began. Two hours a day for three days. That was all the time they had to impress the coaches and change their lives.

Felix and Benji shared a ball and a basket as they warmed up. Benji shot from the foul line. He missed. His form was horrible—elbows out, knees straight, ball held chest high. It was like he forgot how to handle a basketball. Yesterday, at the Times Union Center, he'd looked good. But playing with NBA stars could make anyone look like a legit player.

"I'm nervous." Felix grabbed a rebound, put it back up for an easy lay-up, and then passed the ball back to Benji. "But it's a nice break from spending money."

"You have nothing to worry about." Benji bounced the ball four times, shot, and missed again.

But Felix was worried. He bent down, pretending to tie

his laces, and ran a finger over the red swoosh on his Nike Air Flights. He owned over ten pairs of sneakers now, but these were his favorite—the first he'd bought. The lucky ones.

More players funneled into the gym. Aidan, Jeremy, Luke, and three other kids joined their court. Between them, they had four balls, yet Benji never seemed to be able to grab a rebound. He only got one when Felix fed it to him.

"How many kids do you think are trying out?" Benji asked.

"I don't know." Felix dribbled across the key and sank a left-handed hook shot.

"I heard thirty," Jeremy answered.

"Thirty." Benji let out a big breath. "And how many make the team, like twelve?"

"Last year, only ten." Aidan knocked the ball out of Benji's hands.

A whistle blew. All dribbling and shooting stopped. Balls were returned to the racks, and the hopeful players sprinted to line up in front of Coach Murphy and Coach Orrick. No one walked or hung back. Every minute of try-outs counted.

"For the next three days," Coach Murphy said, "we'll be evaluating you on skills and determination. Both are essential. We will be looking to build the best seventh-grade team for Stirling Middle School. We're not looking for strong, individual players. We're looking for hardworking, motivated players who will make a strong, well-rounded *team*."

Felix's heart pounded against his chest, and it wasn't from the little bit of warm-up. Maybe he wasn't what the team needed.

Coach Murphy blew the whistle again, and thirty minutes of drills began.

Felix had complete control over the ball and was probably the second fastest. He tried not to focus on the other boys, but he couldn't help it. There was only one other kid who handled the ball as well. A kid new to Stirling named Max Wade, who rarely came to open gym because he also played soccer and baseball.

Felix also noticed Benji. He dribbled too high and moved slowly—like he was on a balance beam. At least he didn't lose the ball. Plenty of players had their basketballs ricochet off their knees or sneakers.

"Partner up," Coach yelled, introducing a passing exercise.

Immediately, Felix grabbed Jeremy's sleeve, and they found a spot on the gym floor. Benji jogged over but stopped when he realized Felix already had a partner.

"Sorry," Felix mouthed. Then he turned his attention to the ball, trying not to see Benji's reaction. But he caught enough. No denying that Benji was surprised—and hurt.

There are twenty-seven other players here. He'll find another partner.

And it made sense for Felix to team up with Jeremy. They were both guards. Benji played center or forward. He should be with other big guys.

Coach Murphy ran them through two more drills before allowing a water break.

"There're a lot of good players here," Benji said to Felix as they grabbed their water bottles from the bleachers.

"Yeah."

Felix tried not to overthink it. He tried to focus on *his* game. But as they'd run through the drills, he'd separated everyone into groups: yes, no, and maybe. Max Wade, Jeremy, and Devante landed in the definitely yes gang. Felix felt firmly planted in the maybe category with the majority. It made his stomach hurt.

"At least I'm still the tallest," Benji said. "Maybe that'll give me a chance."

"Maybe." Felix closed his water bottle. He'd said *maybe*, but he'd already put Benji on Team No.

"Thanks for the encouragement." Benji slammed his metal water bottle down on the metal bench. It sounded like a bell ringing.

Felix ran back onto the court. If Benji was going to have an attitude, Felix didn't want to be seen—or heard—with him. They were not a package deal. Benji needed to remember that they were partners for the penny-doubled challenge, not everything else. Not basketball.

The coach had the players join two lines for a two-on-two drill. Felix would rather have had a full scrimmage, but this was nearly as good. He was randomly paired with Max Wade, and they played against Aidan and Luke. Felix and Max scored on their first possession, and the losing duo rotated off the court. Then Felix and Max got new opponents. Max scored another basket, thanks to an assist from Felix. They made a great team, winning six in a row before they came up against Benji and Henry.

"Try not to make me look bad," Benji whispered as he started with the ball. He dribbled twice and took a jump shot. Felix swatted the ball and caused it to miss the basket wildly. Max got the rebound. He dribbled to the top and then dished it off to Felix, who ducked under Benji's meaty arms for an easy lay-up.

"Felix, Max, nice job. Rotate off. Let's change it around," Coach Murphy yelled to them, even though they'd won the matchup.

Felix joined the end of a line, waiting to go back onto the court. A few seconds later, Benji was behind him.

"Nice shot," Benji said, and Felix didn't know if he was sincere. Maybe. But this was tryouts, and everyone was out for himself.

Aidan joined their line. Felix was one away from rotating back in and wanted to distance himself from both Aidan and Benji. He inched forward.

"I'm not going to make it," Benji said. He twisted his foot as if he was digging in the sand.

Felix didn't answer. They would talk about it later. They were neighbors. They shared a driver. Now was not the time.

"Barney, why don't you just give Coach a million dollars," Aidan said. "Or a new car. Then you'll make the team."

"I should," Benji answered quickly, and laughed.

Felix shot him a look. He needed to know Benji wasn't serious.

"Probably doesn't have to be a million. I bet a hundred grand would get you on the team and a starting spot." Aidan wiped his sweaty face on his shirt.

"Probably. But I'm not doing that," Benji said. "You can't bribe a coach."

"This isn't the NBA or the Big Ten. Who cares?"

"I'm not bribing anyone," Benji said.

"Well, looks like Barney is not making the team," Aidan said. Other kids laughed. And it was the last bit of the conversation Felix heard before jumping back onto the court.

Chapter $28

MONDAY, NOVEMBER 15

Benji

Everything hurt, from his toes to his head, but nothing more than Benji's ego. He had no chance of making the basketball team. After the last set of drills, they scrimmaged full-court. Benji didn't score. He didn't get a rebound. And after the first five minutes, he didn't touch the ball at all. His *teammates* had stopped passing to him.

"Must have been a good practice," Reggie said as he drove them to the hotel. "You guys smell worse than ever."

"It was hard," Felix said from the backseat.

"It was ridiculous," Benji added. "There's no way I'm making the team."

"I see." Reggie nodded thoughtfully. "Do you know the guaranteed way to live to be one hundred?"

"How?" Benji asked.

"Eat a Pop-Tart every day for one hundred years." Reggie nodded some more like he'd just shared something brilliant.

"Please stop talking." Benji wasn't in the mood for philosophy or whatever Reggie was spewing.

"You won't make the team if you don't show up," Reggie continued. "Go to tryouts. That's the only way it's going to happen."

"Still not going to happen." Benji leaned his head against the window.

"And you probably won't live to be one hundred, either, but you gotta try."

Reggie dropped them off in front of the hotel. On the elevator, Felix held Freebie's leash and stared at his red-and-white sneakers. It was like he was embarrassed to even be around Benji.

"Bye," Felix said as he ducked out on the fourteenth floor.

Benji threw out his arm to keep the elevator door from closing. "I think I'm going to quit. I'm not going to make the team anyway."

"Really?" Felix stopped and turned around.

"You're not going to talk me out of it?"

Felix shrugged. "You should give it at least one more day," he said, unconvincingly.

"If I don't go to tryouts, I'll have more time to spend money," Benji said.

"True," Felix replied. "But you could have a great day tomorrow and—"

"Stop it. And be honest with me." Benji's throat tightened. "For the past two weeks, we've been completely honest with each other. Right?"

Felix nodded, and his face softened.

Benji stepped out of the elevator and into the hall. "We're sharing this money. We're the only ones who know the truth except for Laura Friendly and the troll and her lawyer goons. We're in this together. We have to count on each other."

"This has nothing to do with basketball." Felix chewed his thumbnail.

"I just want to make the team," Benji said. "Don't you understand that? I need to make the team."

"Why?" Felix asked. "You already have everything. You have friends and two parents and a house, and in a few weeks, you might be an actual millionaire."

"Is that really how you see me? A kid who has it all?" Benji shook his head and jabbed the up button for the elevator. "If you don't make the team, you'll still be an A student. Your mom will probably take you out for ice cream, kiss you on the forehead a thousand times, and tell you how wonderful you are."

"I love basketball. You know that." Felix looked at him like he wasn't sure who he was talking to.

"I love basketball too."

"No." Felix stared at him. "Not really."

Felix's words felt like a slap. Benji had wanted the truth, but now that he had it, things were worse. *Does everyone think I'm a joke?*

"I gotta go." Benji stepped back into the elevator.

When he got to his suite, he went to unlock the door, but it jerked open before the indicator light turned from red to green.

"How did tryouts go?" His dad stood in the doorway with an enormous, hopeful smile.

"I need a shower," Benji answered. "Coach worked us to death."

"How many are trying out? What do you think your chances are?" His dad followed him across the living room.

"There were a lot of guys. So it's hard to say." At least hard to say out loud to his dad.

"Is it still Coach Murphy?" his dad asked. "We used to golf together."

"Huh." Benji walked into his bedroom and peeled off his shirt.

"Maybe I'll give him a call," his dad continued. "See what he's been up to. Maybe invite him to the driving range."

"Dad. Don't." Benji faced his father. He knew his parents did this—called or emailed his teachers and coaches.

He hadn't minded in elementary school. Back then, it had made his life better and easier.

"I won't talk about you or basketball." His dad smiled and winked, confirming that that was all they'd talk about.

"No."

"Okay." His dad shook his head once. "I just know this means a lot to you. You've worked hard and deserve a spot on that team."

Deserve? Do I really?

"I don't expect you to have a career in the NBA," his dad continued. "But sports are important. They teach you teamwork and perseverance. Some of the best friends you'll ever make in your life will be through athletics."

Benji's mind flashed to Felix partnering with Jeremy and putting as much distance between himself and Benji as possible. Except when he blocked Benji's shot. Benji wanted to think Felix wasn't avoiding him on purpose. But he knew better. Sports didn't always result in friendship. It could ruin things too.

"I gotta shower." Benji went into the bathroom.

Benji didn't *deserve* a spot on the team. Lots of guys worked harder than he did. Lots of guys were better players. But he needed it more than them. Not for himself but for his parents. They didn't have a lot to be proud of. He wasn't the best student or a star athlete or a musician or an artist. Didn't all parents expect their kid to excel in one or even two of these areas? If your kid was supersmart and acing tests, it was forgiven that he never hit a home run or scored a goal. If your kid played solos in the band concert, it was okay if he didn't bring home all As. Benji and every kid in public school seemed to be taught that you were good at something. *Everyone is special. Everyone has a gift.*

But what if he wasn't special? Maybe he was one of the few kids born without a natural gift. He'd always be average or below. He was the reason they gave everyone a trophy at the end of the T-ball season, because he'd never earn one of his own.

He took a long, hot shower and tried to wipe away the stench of tryouts.

What good was having millions of dollars at your fingertips if you couldn't use it to buy what you really, *really* needed? Like a spot on the Stirling Middle School basketball team.

Aidan's suggestion popped into his head. *Bribe the coach.* Benji couldn't do that. Not exactly. (It was against Laura Friendly's rules.) But he could still get the coach's attention.

He quickly toweled off, pulled on clean clothes, and ran his fingers through his wet hair. Then he opened his computer and Googled Coach Murphy. There had to be some way to get the guy's attention without writing a million-dollar check (which was not allowed) or having his dad take him golfing. Benji found Coach's social media site—Friendly Connect, as it turned out.

Coach Murphy was a husband, an eighth-grade science teacher, and a dad. He had twin girls, who'd recently turned five and went to Stirling Elementary. Judging from the online pictures and videos, the girls seemed to be obsessed with princesses and unicorns.

The rules said he and Felix couldn't buy gifts for other people. But he could buy food or throw parties—and a parade was a type of moving party, in his opinion.

He opened another Google window and typed *RENT A REAL UNICORN*. He didn't expect anything, but he got a hit. A farm only a few hours away rented out ponies dressed as unicorns for birthday parties and other events.

Benji picked up his phone.

FIRST BANK OF NEW YORK

Current Balance: $2,445,851.63

RECENT TRANSACTIONS

Nov 16, Dreams Come True Party Planning	
	−$11,000.00
Nov 16, Mike's Tacos	−$2,090.00
Nov 16, Little Italy Pizza and Pasta	−$3,080.00
Nov 16, Downtown Donuts	−$1,275.00

Chapter $29

Felix

*B*y *9:00 p.m.*

Coach Murphy had told them the results would be posted on the school's web page by that time. If Coach was going to be punctual, he only had three minutes left.

"Try refreshing it again," Felix said, standing behind Benji.

They'd agreed to wait for the results together—more Benji's idea than Felix's. Felix had been feeling guilty about ignoring Benji on day one of tryouts and could not say no to this simple request. (Thankfully, days two and three had not required any partnering choices.)

Benji didn't have a chance of making the team, but Felix did. And if he was selected, how was he supposed to react in front of Benji and Mr. and Mrs. Porter? He couldn't be happy or excited. And what if he didn't make it? Felix didn't want to consider that option.

Felix had devoted the past three days to basketball and not much else. He'd kept up with his homework, but he and Benji had fallen behind in their daily spending. Felix had bought a few thousand dollars' worth of stuff online. But it was Benji who'd kept them in the game by booking the band Apex-7 for Georgie and Michelle's wedding. It was the only way Felix was able to sleep the past few nights—knowing they had a million-dollar bill coming up on Sunday.

Benji sat on the couch with his computer open on his lap, amazingly calm. Felix paced behind him. Benji's parents certainly weren't calm, though they pretended to be. Mr. Porter leaned against the doorway, fiddling with his phone but mostly staring at Benji. Mrs. Porter flicked channels on the muted TV.

Freebie must have sensed the tension. He lay on the floor but didn't rest his head on his paws as usual. He kept his brown eyes focused on Felix. One of his floppy ears stood up like he was listening intently.

"It's nine," Benji's dad said.

"Refresh it—" Felix began.

"It's up!" Benji interrupted. "Jacob B. Spencer B. Raul E." Benji read the first few names and mumbled a few more.

Then he cursed.

"Benji!" His mom gave a warning.

Felix leaned over Benji's shoulder, needing to see for himself. There were ten names, listed alphabetically by the last initial. His eyes flew through the names. And there it was between Jonas N. and Luke S. With an asterisk next to it.

Felix R.*

What does that mean?

"Benji, you didn't make it?" Mr. Porter asked, but he had to know the answer.

"Of course not." Benji snapped the laptop closed and shoved it into Felix's chest. "Are you really surprised? I suck! I'm sorry, but I suck, and we've all known it. Now it's official. So let's stop pretending."

"Oh, Benji," Mrs. Porter said.

"Did you make the team, Felix?" Mr. Porter asked.

"I'm not sure." It was the truth. He opened the laptop again and set it on the dining table. He needed to know what the star meant.

"He made it," Benji said. "His name is on the list."

"Congratulations," Mr. Porter said. "I'm happy for you." Felix thought he sounded sincere.

"Benji, there's always next season," Mrs. Porter said. "Michael Jordan didn't make his varsity team when he first tried, and look at how that worked out."

"He played JV instead, and he didn't make varsity because he wasn't tall yet. I'm already the biggest guy." Benji ran both hands over his head.

"You gave it your best shot. That's all anyone can ask of

you." Mr. Porter squeezed Benji's shoulder. Then he paused as if waiting for Benji to reply.

"And my best isn't good enough." Benji went into his room and slammed the door.

Felix focused on the web page, reading it from top to bottom. Beneath the practice schedule, there was a definition for the asterisk.

See me on Thursday.

Thursday, November 18

Felix knocked on the open classroom door to get Coach Murphy's attention. It was twenty minutes before school, and Coach stood alone at the dry-erase board, writing questions with a blue marker.

"Good morning, Felix. Come in." Coach capped his marker.

Felix didn't know if he should take a seat. He hoped not to be here that long. He hoped for a simple explanation, like *You made the team, but your mom forgot to sign the medical form.*

"Good morning." He decided to stand.

"I need to ask you a question before I can give you a spot on the team." Coach crossed his arms and drew a big breath. "Did you have anything to do with the bribe that was sent to my kids' school?"

"What?" Felix hadn't expected this—or, more accurately, didn't want to think it possible. He looked at the banking app almost hourly. He knew Benji had made some charges to party places, which could have been for anything—for the wedding, for their lunch period, for an actual party. The goal was to spend money, so Felix didn't question it.

He didn't want to question it.

"Yesterday, three 'unicorns' and a small army of princesses showed up at my daughters' elementary school." Coach made air quotes around the word *unicorns*.

Benji hadn't ridden with Felix to school yesterday morning. He'd said there was something he had to take care of. Something important. Felix didn't make a big deal out of it. He just enjoyed his chance to ride in the Bugatti.

"Did you know anything about it?" Coach Murphy asked.

Felix's heart sped up, and his legs wobbled. He wasn't sure how to answer. Coach's stare made him feel like he was hooked to a lie detector.

"I . . . um . . ." He took a deep breath. Did Coach know Benji had set it up? Or, if Felix mentioned Benji, would he rat out his friend?

"You're looking very nervous." Coach narrowed his eyes. Did he also mean Felix was looking very guilty?

"I didn't have anything to do with it," Felix finally said, and it was the truth.

"But Benji Porter did."

"I don't know."

Coach said nothing. He just waited, standing completely still. But Felix was a pro at staying quiet and motionless.

Finally, Coach Murphy spoke. "You can't buy your way onto a basketball team."

"Yes, sir."

"I want a hardworking team that I can trust," the coach continued. "If you swear you were not involved with the scheme, I'd like to offer you a spot."

"I swear."

Noises filled the hallway as students chatted and headed to homerooms.

"Welcome to the team, Felix." Coach uncrossed his arms and offered Felix a handshake. "I'll see you at practice this afternoon."

Relief washed over Felix. This was what he wanted, to be on Stirling Middle School's seventh-grade team. But he also felt pressure in his chest. Benji hadn't gotten what he wanted.

"Coach, can I ask you a question?" Felix stepped closer so the few students trickling into the room wouldn't hear.

"Shoot."

"Would Benji have made the team if he hadn't . . ." Felix didn't want to say *bribe*.

"No. He wouldn't have made the team. But that's the least of his problems."

Chapter $30

THURSDAY AND FRIDAY, NOVEMBER 18 AND 19

Benji

Benji walked out of the principal's office. This time, he hadn't been given five million dollars. He'd been given three days' detention for violation of the Stirling code of conduct. Though he technically never confessed to any code of conduct violations. He'd only admitted to showing up at the elementary school with unicorns.

As Benji stepped into the cafeteria for lunch, someone grabbed his shoulder. He turned to see Felix.

"You tried to bribe the coach?" Felix asked. "What's wrong with you?"

"What do you care? You made the team." Benji slipped around Felix and headed toward the station of pizza and tacos. He didn't want to talk about this anymore. He didn't want to be at school—and he had an extra hour for detention coming his way.

"But I almost didn't." Felix followed him.

"But you did!" Benji shouted. His eyes burned, and he took a deep breath to keep his voice steady. "I never had a shot. And you didn't even want to be my partner at tryouts, Felix. I had to do something."

"That's not true," Felix said.

"Why bother lying now? It's over." Benji took a seat at the end of the table and put his head in his hands. "Just leave me alone."

He could feel Felix lingering. Benji closed his eyes and tried to wish him away.

"I'm sorry you didn't make the team," Felix said. "But what you did was stupid." Benji didn't need to look to know that Felix had walked off.

• • •

After detention, Benji had his mom pick him up and take him home. Not to the hotel. But home. She was not happy about the alleged bribe, but since she had to get back to work, she didn't make it a big deal, and his dad was traveling. On Friday, his mom let him miss school when he lied about diarrhea. (No one ever wants to admit to having the runs, so it's the best sickness lie going.)

Felix didn't call or text Benji either day. He was probably too busy with basketball and school and spending. Benji didn't care.

November 19

So I didn't make the basketball team. I'm very disappointed, but I will practice, practice, practice, and I bet I get on the eighth-grade team. When I found out that I didn't make it, I thought that was the end, but my mom convinced me I could try again.

I have detention for a few days because of a misunderstanding. I messed up when I tried to do something nice for Coach Murphy. It's all okay now.

School is fine too. I forgot to finish a project on Greek culture. I'll make up the work. No problem.

Over and out,
Benji

Saturday, November 20

That morning, Felix finally called.

"Hey, where are you?"

"Home."

"We need to spend some money," Felix reminded him. "We're falling behind."

The only money Benji had spent in the last twenty-four hours was on in-app purchases. He didn't need anything else.

"I'm not feeling up to it." Benji opened the fridge and just stared at the food. "I have diarrhea."

"Come on, Benji. I need your help."

"No, you don't." Benji yanked out the milk and dropped a yogurt on the newly refinished floors. "We can each spend money on our own. We have our own lives. Don't we? Nowhere in the rules does it say we have to do this together."

Benji cleaned up the mess and waited for a reply. Something like *But we're partners.* Or *It's fun to do this together.* Or *I'm sorry I ignored you at tryouts, and everyone thinks I'm the nice guy, but I can be a jerk, too.*

But Felix didn't say anything. And when Benji's phone buzzed with an incoming text message, he hung up with a quick goodbye.

ALMA: Hi. It's Alma.

His stomach flipped, he felt dizzy, and he started to sweat. She had the same effect on him as the Dare Devil Dive ride at Six Flags. He didn't reply immediately, not because he was playing it cool. Quite the opposite. His hands were shaking, and he didn't want to mess this up. Ultimately, he decided to follow her lead.

BENJI: Hi

She *did* reply instantly, which was good because his heart couldn't take the wait.

ALMA: Do you want to get ice cream?

ALMA: I have a BOGO coupon.

His instinct was to offer to pay. He could buy her all the ice cream in the store. He could fly her to Italy and get fancy gelato. He could buy a cow, and they could make their own ice cream. *(How long does it take to make ice cream?)* He knew she wouldn't appreciate any of those offers.

And her offer was already perfect.

BENJI: Sure

ALMA: 1pm at Sprinkles???

BENJI: OK

He ran upstairs and took a shower. After he got dressed, he checked his phone, worried Alma might cancel or text *JK*. But she hadn't said anything. Felix had sent at least twenty messages. Most begging him to waste the day spending a million dollars. It was all a business transaction. Nothing more.

Alma had warned him that all the money might make it hard to tell who his real friends were. He'd never imagined she could be talking about Felix.

At five minutes to one, Benji stood outside Sprinkles. His mom had dropped him off early—no chance he was going to be late. The place was empty. Not many people were getting ice cream in the middle of November.

Alma arrived with her sister. Ava went into a beauty supply store in another part of the shopping center, leaving Benji and Alma alone. Like a date. Or maybe like friends. It didn't matter.

Alma wore a long black winter coat and a fuzzy purple hat. Benji had never seen anyone so cute. He wanted to tell her but chickened out.

"Hey. Let's get some ice cream," she said, waving her coupon.

He pulled open the door and followed her to the counter. It was one of those places that custom-creates the ice cream, mixing the base with candy or nuts or fruit. *(Fruit in ice cream. What a waste!)* Alma got vanilla with bananas, cherries, and chocolate flakes. *(It's okay when she does it.)* Benji ordered caramel with Cap'n Crunch mixed in.

"Will you yell at me if I try to pay?" he asked when they got to the register.

"Yes." Alma flashed him a smile as she gave the cashier her coupon and a ten-dollar bill.

They took a seat at a metal table at the back of the shop. Benji stirred his ice cream and took a small bite. Alma sang to herself as she took a few mouthfuls.

"How are you?" she asked.

"Great." He smiled.

"Really? You weren't at school yesterday, and on Thursday, I saw you and Felix fighting at lunch."

"Geez, are you stalking me?" He was kind of flattered that she'd noticed he was absent. "I'm kidding."

She raised her eyebrows and pulled her lips to one side.

"Felix and I aren't fighting. I did something stupid, but I don't know why he's upset. It didn't affect him." *Not really.*

"And he's not perfect either." Benji forced down a spoonful. "It's complicated."

"Because of the money?" She handed him a napkin. He wiped his face from chin to forehead, worried he was covered in ice cream.

"I didn't make the basketball team." He looked at the wall behind her as he spoke.

"That stinks." She touched his arm lightly, and when he looked at her hand, she pulled it away.

"I don't even like basketball much." He stirred his ice cream again and again. It resembled a chunky, disgusting milk shake at this point.

"Then why did you try out?" she asked, her voice not sounding sympathetic anymore.

"Look at me. I'm huge. I'm supposed to play basketball. And both my parents played. It's important."

"Doesn't sound important to you."

"I just want to be good at something."

"You know what you should do?" Alma tapped the table, excited. "You should audition for the spring musical. We're doing *Shrek*."

"You can't be serious." He snorted. "I don't do theater."

"Why not? You're practically guaranteed a spot. Hardly any boys audition. Maybe you'll even be Shrek."

"Do you think I'm an ogre?" He looked her in the eyes, and the hair on his arms stood up.

"With the right makeup, you could pass for an ogre."

"Wait. You get to wear makeup in the musical? Then I'm totally in," he said jokingly. "When are auditions?"

"Soon. In December." She smiled. "I bet you'll look good in green."

He wished he was painted green right now because he could feel his face go totally red.

"I'll think about it."

Alma finished her ice cream as they talked about the drama club fundraiser. Benji promised to volunteer and supply pizza. Then they discussed movies and books—well, books that had been made into movies. They didn't talk about basketball or money or Felix. A little-kid birthday party came into the shop—raising the noise level tenfold—and Benji and Alma still sat and talked.

Ava walked in just after two-thirty carrying a yellow bag and told Alma it was time to go.

Benji gathered their empty bowls and threw them out. It was the least he could do.

Alma pulled on her fuzzy hat and zipped up her coat. "This was fun. We should hang out more."

"Absolutely. What are you doing tomorrow?" Benji asked, half joking.

"Nothing," Alma said, and Benji's heart leaped. Was she half joking too? Was she suggesting a second date? Wait, was this a first date? What made something a date? He didn't move because he didn't know how to reply. His brain was overloaded with questions and no answers.

"You okay?"

"Yeah. Yeah." He shook his head and forced his brain to focus. "I have to go to a wedding tomorrow. Felix's sister is getting married, and we've got an epic surprise planned." He didn't want to see Felix and didn't really care about the wedding, but he was looking forward to the Apex-7 concert he'd arranged.

"Do you want to come?" he asked.

"Sure." And with that answer, the Apex-7 concert dropped to second place of things he was looking forward to tomorrow.

Chapter $31

SUNDAY, NOVEMBER 21

Felix

Felix wore a dark suit and his Nike Flights and stood next to his mom and sister, smiling until his cheeks hurt and his bottom lip felt like it might split open.

"One more," said the photographer. Felix knew the one-more promise was a lie because he'd heard it repeated three times already.

After what seemed like a few million pictures, the wedding finally began. Michelle and her father went down the aisle first. When Georgie grabbed Felix's elbow, her arm shook. He hadn't been nervous, but seeing his sister jittery made his stomach flip, and all he had to do was walk her to the front.

"You look beautiful," he whispered as they stepped onto the white carpet.

"I might throw up," she replied, which made him feel queasy.

The seats were full. Felix scanned the crowd as they slowly walked to the front. He saw Laura Friendly. That was a shock. He'd sent an invitation but never expected her to show up. Then he spotted Mr. and Mrs. Porter, Reggie, Alma, and the back of Benji's head. How long was Benji going to ignore him? Did he really think they didn't need to work together?

Yesterday, Felix had done well on his own. He'd rented out the South Bank Speedway and driven the Bugatti (how many twelve-year-olds could say that!), with a nervous Reggie riding shotgun. He more coasted than drove, taking about ten minutes to get around the quarter-mile track. And when he left Freebie alone in the car for two seconds, the dog chewed the steering wheel, thus ensuring they weren't getting their security deposit back. He'd ordered ugly designer clothes from Bloomingdale's. He'd bought a time capsule that would be sent up into space. And he now owned seven Stetson Diamante Premier cowboy hats—one for every day of the week.

After the ceremony (where no one vomited), Felix endured a few more pictures before joining the party. Tuxedoed waiters passed around hors d'oeuvres and drinks. Felix wandered around the ballroom, looking for Benji, but bumped into Laura Friendly first.

"This is quite an event," she said, sipping a glass of champagne. "I assume you paid."

"We did. And it's completely within the rules," he said defensively. "Everything checked out by Mr. Trulz."

FIRST BANK OF NEW YORK

Current Balance: $2,238,116.32

RECENT TRANSACTIONS	
Nov 20, Bloomingdale's	−$13,645.80
Nov 20, In the Stars Time Capsules	−$9,999.00
Nov 20, Stetson Hats	−$45,118.08
Nov 20, South Bank Speedway (Track Rental–2 Hours)	−$75,000.00

"I'm sure," she said. "You strike me as a rule-follower. Someone who doesn't color outside the lines. Someone who tells the teacher that she forgot to assign homework. Someone who would return money if he found it lying on the street."

He wasn't sure if he should say thank you or be insulted.

"You've thrown a lovely reception. Enjoy it." She raised her glass like a toast. "My wedding was a disaster and even included a literal tornado. We hid in a bathroom for a half hour. I should have seen it as a sign of things to come."

"You're married?" Felix asked. He'd read her book on business and getting ahead. It didn't say much about her personal life and never mentioned a husband.

"Was," she answered quickly. "Lasted less than a presidential term, though I'm still paying for it. *Literally.*"

"Is that what you'd do over? Not get married?"

"What are you talking about, my boy?" she asked, grabbing another glass of champagne from a waiter.

"You said all the money in the world couldn't buy you a do-over," Felix said, reminding her of their conversation at the basketball game.

Her face fell. "No. While my marriage to Tom was a failure, that's not what I want to do over."

She shook her head. Felix didn't know if she was going to say more, and he didn't get a chance to find out because the DJ's voice boomed over the speakers.

"Ladies and gentlemen, please gather around the dance floor as we introduce the wedding party."

Then the wedding planner grabbed Felix's shoulder. "You're needed now."

"Off you go," Ms. Friendly said.

The DJ introduced the bridesmaids and bridesmen, Michelle's parents, Felix and his mom, and finally, Georgie and Michelle. Then the music started, and the brides had their first official dance. Halfway through the song, the wedding party was asked to join them, and Felix's mom dragged him onto the wooden dance floor. No one had warned him he'd have to dance at this thing.

"At first, I wasn't sure about this wedding," his mom said as they slowly turned in circles.

She must have seen the shock on Felix's face because she quickly added, "Not the marriage. The *wedding*. The big, fancy, expensive wedding."

"Oh."

"But I'm glad you did this. It's nice. And I know you and Georgie didn't get a lot of *nice*, growing up." She smiled, but her eyes looked sad. "Well, you're still growing up. But I mean, you've both missed out on things."

"Not really." He didn't have as much as Benji and most of the other kids in his class, but he wasn't hungry or homeless—at least not yet.

"I wanted to give you more. Like new clothes, vacations, big Christmases with hundreds of presents, a cell phone."

"A cell phone would have been nice," he teased her.

She kissed his cheek and then wiped away the lipstick she'd left behind.

When the song ended, everyone was ordered to their assigned tables, but Georgie pulled Felix aside.

"Thank you again, Felix. This is the wedding of my dreams." She squeezed his hand and looked like she might cry.

"You're welcome."

"And I can't wait to see what surprise is next. Benji let it slip that you have something big for us." She leaned forward and whispered. "It's a house, isn't it?"

The band!

"No! It's not a house."

"I'll act surprised." She wasn't listening to him. "You've done so much already. I can't believe ... I can't believe more of my dreams are coming true."

"Georgie, there's no house."

She smiled and winked at him. Then Michelle was suddenly at Georgie's side, pulling her to the head table.

Felix ran to find Benji. "We need to talk."

Benji sighed heavily and pushed back his chair. He groaned as he got up from the table like it took tremendous strength and energy.

"Is the band here?" Felix asked when they'd stepped out of earshot.

"Yep. They're setting up in the courtyard." Benji gestured with his thumb.

Felix could see men carrying equipment through the hallway. "And it cost a million?"

"With expenses, it'll be one-point-one million." Benji spun his finger in mock celebration. "Awesome, right?"

"No." Every cell in Felix's body was telling him to pull the plug. But they were close to winning. After the wedding and the concert, they'd have less than a million left. This was the end game. He could buy Georgie and Michelle a house in December.

"This is not what Georgie really wants," he said.

"Well, life is full of disappointments." Benji pushed past Felix.

Chapter $32

Benji

This will be the best part of the wedding. This will be what people remember, Benji thought and only partially believed.

Then he tapped his finger against the microphone. "Excuse me. May I have your attention?"

The room quieted, and all eyes snapped to him. He glanced at *his* table. Alma gave him a little wave, and his ears felt suddenly warm. Laura Friendly leaned her head on her palm, probably bored. Reggie gave him a thumbs-up. Benji's mom smiled and seemed to be having a good time, but his dad looked like he was waiting for a dentist to drill holes in each one of his teeth.

"I'm Benji Porter. I'm friends with the bride's brother, Felix." *Friend* was a strong word, but now wasn't the time to get a thesaurus.

Ms. Rannells nudged Felix forward to join Benji at the DJ stand.

"Felix and I have arranged a special gift for the bride and bride," Benji continued.

Georgie and Michelle stepped to the edge of the dance floor, arms linked. Michelle wore a snug red wedding dress, and Georgie definitely looked prettier in her gown than Felix had looked. They'd been smiling all day, but now they somehow smiled even more brightly.

"It's a little something to make this special day *extra* special. Like sprinkles on an ice cream sundae."

The crowd chuckled.

Benji leaned over to Felix and whispered, "Do you want to say anything?"

Felix shook his head but then murmured, "Congratulations."

"Okay." Benji turned back to the guests. "Georgie. Michelle. If you're ready for this, follow us to the courtyard."

Benji handed the microphone back to the DJ and led the way out of the ballroom. Felix walked beside him, looking more sick than happy. When they got to the glass doors that led outside, Benji grabbed one handle, and he motioned for Felix to take the other. Benji counted down from three, and then they pulled the doors wide.

The music started on cue.

"I've been waiting my whole life for this moment," sang Logan Jeffers, the leader of Apex-7.

Georgie screamed and cursed, but in a happy way. Her hands flew to her face, and she jumped again and again. (Benji knew that wasn't easy in a wedding dress.)

"Get in there," Benji said. "This is for you."

The happy couple danced their way toward the low stage where Apex-7 was performing.

The rest of the guests pushed closer to see what was happening. More screams flowed back through the crowd when they realized it was the actual Grammy-winning artists and not a cover band.

"Georgie didn't want this, huh?" Benji said to Felix.

Felix shrugged and looked unconvinced.

They continued to hold the doors open as the guests streamed past. Nearly every one of them had a cell phone out, recording the epic event.

When Alma got to the door, she shrieked.

"Is that really Apex-7? I love them."

"I can introduce you later," Benji said like it was no big deal, though he hadn't met them yet.

He made his way inside the courtyard with Alma. Someone else could hold the door. She grabbed his hand and pulled him toward the front.

Alma didn't let go of his hand as a second song started. They bounced and swayed (not quite dancing, but kind of).

He didn't even worry about how sweaty his palms were—at least, not too much.

Suddenly, someone yanked the back of Benji's suit coat. He turned to see his parents. Alma dropped his hand.

His dad said something, but the music was too loud. Benji could tell from the lines in his dad's forehead that it wasn't a compliment.

His dad leaned into his face. "Did you pay for this?" He gestured to the stage.

Benji shrugged and pointed to his ears, pretending he still couldn't hear.

The song came to an end, and Logan Jeffers tried to offer a toast to the happy couple. But Benji's dad had the guests' attention.

"How much did this cost?" Benji's dad asked, not giving up.

"It's our gift to the brides," Benji said.

Alma stepped back, as did everyone else. A circle had formed around Benji and his parents, like on the playground when kids find a dead bird.

"How much?" Spit flew as his dad yelled.

"It's my money." Out of the corner of his eye, Benji saw Felix. His dad followed his gaze.

"What did this cost?" Benji's dad asked Felix.

Felix turned white, and Benji thought he might tip over.

You don't have to answer, Benji tried to say telepathically.

"What's going on?" Georgie stepped into the circle.

"I want to know what they paid for this private concert," Benji's dad said. "A million? Two million?"

"No way." Georgie forced a laugh. "I bet Jeffers is just friends with Ms. Friendly."

Georgie scanned the room, probably searching for the tech billionaire, who was nowhere in sight.

"Right, Felix? You wouldn't spend millions on a concert." She nodded nervously.

Felix's gaze dropped to the floor.

"Oh my God, you did." Georgie's face fell. "What did you spend?"

The room was completely quiet. No one moved, but plenty of people held up cell phones, still recording the event.

"Felix!" Georgie snapped.

Benji could almost imagine the apology forming in Felix's brain. Felix was an expert at saying *I'm sorry*. He'd had lots of practice. But Benji knew that this time it wouldn't be enough.

"It doesn't matter! It's our money. If we want to spend a million dollars on a concert, we can!" Benji yelled suddenly, even surprising himself.

Gasps echoed through the crowd.

"Oh, Benji," his mom said.

Georgie continued to focus on only Felix. "You spent a

million on this? While your family doesn't have a house or a decent car."

"It was my idea," Benji practically shouted. "Felix didn't want to do it." Benji's parents were already upset and thought he was a screw-up. Maybe he could keep Felix from experiencing the same fate.

"What were you thinking?" Georgie grabbed Felix by the shoulders. He still didn't look up.

"Shh," Michelle said, and put a hand on Georgie's back. "Shh. It'll be okay."

But Georgie didn't stop.

"I can't afford to go to the dentist unless I work overtime at my crappy job, and you spent a million dollars on a concert? What's wrong with you? When did you become so selfish?"

Georgie's eyes filled with tears, and some escaped, running down her blotchy cheeks. Michelle gently wiped them away. Then Felix's mom appeared at her side. She held Georgie's hand and whispered something in her ear. Georgie only cried harder before the three of them walked out.

"I'm sorry!" Felix yelled to them, no longer able to hold in the apology.

"This all ends now." Benji's dad held out his hand. "Give me your debit card, your wallet, your phone. All of it."

"Jack, let's talk at home," his mom said.

"It's been three weeks, and he's wasted all his money. No

more. I should have done this on day one." He looked like Bruce Banner, ready to turn into the Hulk. His hands curled into fists. His neck grew in size. His face got red, not green.

Benji's mom stepped in. "We're leaving."

"Okay," Benji said. Then he turned to Felix. He couldn't talk to him right now, but if he could have, he'd have said: *You and me. We're all alone in this mess. But we'll get through it. I promise, buddy.*

Felix nodded once like he understood.

FIRST BANK OF NEW YORK

Current Balance: $992,996.32

RECENT TRANSACTIONS

Nov 21, Concert Services Delivered (Apex-7)
                                    −$1,100,000.00

Nov 21, Capital Weddings   −$140,000.00

Nov 21, Blake's Professional Photography −$5,000.00

Nov 21, Good Dog (Dog-Sitting)   −$120.00

Chapter $33

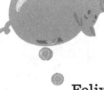

Felix

Felix, against his better judgment, clicked on another link. This post was titled "Billionaire Brats." They might have come across as brats, but they certainly weren't billionaires. The video showed Benji and his parents shouting at Georgie's wedding. Then a British man appeared on the screen and criticized Benji and Felix. He called them spoiled, entitled, wasteful Americans.

"Turn that off," his mom said as she walked through the living room of their hotel suite.

"One second."

"Furthermore," the British man with white-blond hair said, "only tone-deaf American parents would allow such behavior. These misfits should be removed from the home, and their parents sentenced to—"

That was enough for Felix. He muted that site and

Googled *billionaire brats*. He hoped someone would come to their defense. Maybe even Laura Friendly. Instead of finding what he wanted, he came across an ad offering the domain name BillionaireBratz.com for $65,000. He bought it.

"Please, get off the computer," his mom said. "Are you okay? You don't look good." She poured him a glass of orange juice and then touched his forehead like she was taking his temperature.

"I'm fine. How is Georgie?"

After the wedding had ended abruptly, Felix had gone back to his hotel room. His mom hadn't returned until almost 10:00 p.m., and she'd said she was tired and they'd talk in the morning. He'd tried to call Benji, but no one answered. Felix assumed—or hoped—Benji was under some kind of house arrest. He didn't want to think Benji was still mad.

"Georgie's confused. Honestly, we all are. She knows she should be grateful for what you've given her, and she is. But other things would make their lives easier, that they would've appreciated even more."

"Like a house," he mumbled.

"I don't expect you to buy your sister a house." His mom patted his hand. "She'll be okay. You need to talk to her when she gets back from Vermont."

He nodded. It wasn't their official honeymoon, but

Georgie and Michelle were heading to Michelle's family for Thanksgiving week.

"I gotta take Freebie out." *And go see Benji.* Felix got up, grabbed a leash, and clipped it to Freebie.

"We're not done talking." His mom stepped in front of him, and when she got a look at his outfit, she raised her eyebrows. "And what are you wearing?"

"Frodo's pants." He also had on a Champion sweatshirt and his red-and-white Nike Air Flights. But he knew it was the short brown velvet pants that got her attention.

She let out a loud breath. "Perfect example. You're not responsible with the money. It needs to stop. I want your debit card." She held out her hand.

He didn't want to give it up. He shouldn't. But the look in her eyes made it clear; this was not a choice. He slipped it out of his sweatshirt pocket and laid it in her palm.

He took a deep breath. *I can call Trulz and get another one.* And the account number was saved on his computer. He could still shop online. They only had a little over $900,000 left. It could be done.

"Thank you."

Freebie pulled on the leash.

"Can I take him out now?"

"There's one more thing." She rubbed his arms like she was trying to warm him up. "I'm quitting my job at Express Services. I'm giving my two weeks' notice today."

Why would you do that? He fought back the words. He knew why she'd do that. Her son was a spoiled "billionaire brat" who'd spent a million on a concert that had lasted twenty minutes.

"I thought about this a lot last night," she continued. "I can't work both jobs with my classes starting soon. I tried to ask my boss to cut back my hours at the warehouse—work only weekends—but she said no. If I want to get my degree, this is the only way it's going to happen."

"Mom, you can't quit. We can't afford it." With two jobs, things were already tight at the end of each month. They could only buy essentials at the grocery store, like milk, bread, and canned soup. Sometimes even the laundry money ran out. What would they do without half her income?

"Don't worry about our finances. That's my job. Okay?" She tilted her head and nodded, obviously wanting him to agree with her. But he couldn't.

"I am worried," he mumbled.

"Felix, you may be the millionaire, but I'm the adult."

"You're not acting like an adult!" He hated himself for saying that, but how else could he get through to her? "Half the time we go to the store, you can't even afford potato chips. And now you're quitting your job. That's stupid."

"Watch it!" She held up a finger in warning. "If you want

potato chips, you can buy potato chips. With your money. Please don't act like you're starving and homeless."

"If you quit your job, I might be." *And if we don't win this challenge, I one hundred percent will be.*

"Enough, Felix!" she yelled, and he flinched. She pressed her fingertips to her eyes and shook her head. His mom never raised her voice. Neither of them knew how to react. They stood silently for what felt like ten minutes.

"Finish getting ready for school," she finally said.

"Okay." He pulled Freebie toward the door. "I'm sorry, Mom." *But please don't quit your job.*

"I will always do what is best for us, Felix. I hope you know that."

He nodded without looking back. How could she do what was best when she didn't know what was really happening?

Freebie and Felix rode the elevator down to the first floor. The dog sat patiently until the doors slid open. Then he dragged Felix across the lobby and outside to his favorite small patch of grass near the Grand Regency sign.

As Freebie sniffed for the perfect spot, Felix heard someone call his name.

"Felix. Felix. How much money have you spent?" A man was recording Felix and Freebie on a cell phone.

"I don't know."

"Have you invested any of the money? Have you given

any to charity? Are you wasting it all?" The man hurled question after question.

Felix focused on Freebie, who was squatting in the number two position. Felix reached into his coat pocket for a plastic baggie to pick it up.

Ugh. He'd forgotten a poop bag.

"Come on, Freebie." Felix tugged on the leash. He needed to get out of there.

"You just going to leave that?" the man asked. "Do you care about anything?"

"Um . . . I don't have a bag," Felix replied.

"You could use a hundred-dollar bill." The man laughed and kept the camera focused on Felix.

"Hey! Hey!" Felix turned to see Reggie jogging toward them. "Leave the kid alone."

"We're just talking." The man held up his hands. "I'm from the *Daily Beat.*"

"Felix, let's go." Reggie put an arm over Felix's shoulder and led him back inside the hotel. "You good, boss?"

"Yeah. Thanks." Felix motioned toward the elevator. "I'm going to check on Benji."

Felix needed to talk to him. Benji would make a joke about the reporter. He'd think the billionaire brats videos were funny (and he'd be impressed that Felix bought the domain name). He'd suggest they hire a plane and have BBQ in North Carolina for dinner. He'd promise that they'd still win the penny-doubled challenge, and that Felix's mom's decision to quit was no biggie. *We've got over a week and less than a million left. Relax, buddy.*

Felix stepped off the elevator on the fifteenth floor, knowing Benji would make him feel better. If they could just talk for two minutes. But when Felix knocked, no one answered.

Chapter $34

Benji

Benji "agreed" to the Monday lunch meeting because he didn't have a choice. Maybe this would make his parents happy. Nothing he did ever seemed to. That was true before the money and doubly true after. But maybe on December 2, they'd understand.

His mom sat to his left, his dad to his right, and across from him was Mr. Rubin—a financial adviser. Benji had lied and told Mr. Rubin they had three million left in their bank account. He flashed him a screenshot of the banking app from last week and played it off like today's balance. And as Benji ate a salad drenched in ranch, then chicken and rice, and then sorbet for dessert, the man explained how, with the right strategy, Benji could pay for his education and retire by the age of thirty.

Who wants to work until they're thirty?

But Benji politely nodded and listened and kept most of

his attention on his dad, who smiled every time Mr. Rubin said *annuity,* or *compound interest,* or *low-risk.*

As the adults drank coffee, Mr. Rubin took a phone call and excused himself from the table.

"We should have had this meeting on the first day," Benji's dad said, folding his hands on the white tablecloth.

Benji nodded like a bobblehead doll on a dashboard.

"But better late than never. We can move the money to a Flyers Account this afternoon." His dad stared hard, like he knew Benji was going to object.

"I don't think I'm allowed to transfer money," Benji reminded his dad.

"My lawyer disagrees. If the money is in your name, it can't be held hostage by a financial institution or anyone else, including Laura Friendly. We're going to the bank now."

"Not today. Um . . . I should go to school." He wanted to see Felix.

"Let's do it before we leave for Aruba." His mom folded her napkin and placed it on the table. "Get everything taken care of so we can enjoy our Thanksgiving break."

"Fine. Let's go." Benji stood up, and the water glasses rattled. He didn't want to play this game anymore.

Less than thirty minutes later, they were at the bank. The four of them sat in the office with the bank manager, who explained that Benji could not make a withdrawal. *Shocker!*

"I'm sorry," the manager said, without sounding sorry at all. (He had sounded sorry the first seven times he had said it.)

"It's my client's money," Mr. Rubin said.

"It's a custodial account," the manager explained again.

"We've hired a lawyer," Benji's dad threatened.

"It doesn't matter. Come back with a lawyer. Come back with a team of lawyers. The only way you will get access to the money is if you come back with masks and guns." He swore under his breath and then apologized. Bank managers were probably not supposed to suggest armed robbery as a way of doing business. "Is there anything else I can assist you with?"

Tuesday, November 23

Benji and his parents waited at gate B48 for their evening flight to Aruba. He could have flown them in a private jet, but no way would they have agreed to that.

His parents still hadn't given Benji back his phone. It was home on the counter. This was part of his punishment—no phone, no computer, no contact with anyone in the outside world. And no debit card.

When his dad went to get Starbucks, Benji took the opportunity to appeal to his mom. He needed to call Felix. She frowned at first and then handed over her phone.

"Hello?" Felix answered.

"Hey, buddy. It's me." Benji wandered out of his mom's eavesdropping zone.

"Where are you? You haven't spent any money since the wedding."

Felix's first thought is always money. No *How are you? Everything okay?* Benji tried not to take it personally.

"I'm at the airport. We're going to Aruba for Thanksgiving. Tradition," Benji explained.

"Everything is falling apart," Felix said. "Mr. Palomino demanded we stop the pizza and tacos, doughnuts, everything. I think it's because of the video from the wedding. Have you seen it?"

"Yeah." Benji stood in front of a large window and watched workers load suitcases into the belly of an airplane.

"I skipped basketball practice today to see Mr. Trulz and get a new debit card because my mom took away the original one. I probably lost my place on the team. Then I went to rent a blimp, and it was too windy to take it up."

Benji snorted.

"Are you laughing?" Felix asked.

"No."

"It's not funny," Felix said. "My mom quit her job at the warehouse."

"You're right. None of this is funny." Benji leaned his forehead against the cold glass. His parents thought he was the world's biggest screw-up. Everyone saw the boys as selfish jerks. Benji really just wanted it all to be over.

"Don't you get it? I have to win. My family needs this money."

"I get it! What if we just tell our parents but swear them to secrecy?" Benji suggested. It was the most obvious solution, even if it was bending (*okay, breaking*) a rule.

"No." Felix sighed into the phone. "I'll figure this out on my own. We've only got about nine hundred thousand left. Just don't tell anyone. Don't mess this up."

"I won't." *What's another seven days of my parents thinking I'm the world's biggest screw-up?* Benji looked across the crowded airport. His dad was back at their seats. He pointed at Benji and motioned for him to rejoin them. Benji turned away quickly, pretending not to notice.

"And you don't have to do it alone," Benji continued. "I'll be back Sunday. We'll skip school. Fly to Hawaii and blow the rest of the money. We'll win, Felix." Benji tried to sound believable.

"Okay," Felix replied softly. "I'll see you on Sunday."

Benji felt a tap on his shoulder.

"Gotta go." Benji hung up the phone and turned to face his dad. Strangely, his dad didn't look upset or even disappointed. He tilted his head and smiled.

Benji handed over the phone. "What's going on?"

His dad held up a folded newspaper and pointed to an article.

"The band—Apex-7—they're refunding your money. Most of it, anyway. They're keeping a few thousand for expenses, but they're returning over one million dollars. I think the social-media pressure got to them. They took advantage of a couple of naive kids. That's not the publicity anyone wants."

"That's good news," Benji said through gritted teeth. "Can I call Felix and tell him?"

"No. You two need a break from each other. He seems like a decent kid, but together you're trouble."

Wrong, Benji thought. *We're not trouble. We're in trouble.*

FIRST BANK OF NEW YORK

Current Balance: $1,936,636.10

RECENT TRANSACTIONS

Nov 23, Concert Services Delivered (Apex-7)
+$1,080,000.00

Nov 23, To: Reggie Fazil (Payroll–Dog-Sitting)
−$1,000.00

Nov 23, To: Reggie Fazil (Payroll–Chauffeur)
−$6,727.50

Nov 23, Nordstrom   −$12,365.00

Chapter $35

THURSDAY, NOVEMBER 25

Felix

Felix's mom insisted on cooking Thanksgiving dinner in their apartment, even though the hotel offered an all-you-can-eat buffet. And with Georgie and Michelle in Vermont, she was happy to extend the guest list. Felix invited Reggie—who felt like family—and Laura Friendly. He needed to try one more time to get her to change the rules. His mom had quit one of her jobs, and Apex-7 had returned over a million dollars.

The guests arrived at noon. Laura Friendly showed up with a massive bouquet of flowers and a bottle of wine.

"I have two rules for my Thanksgiving dinner," Felix's mom said. "Number one: no talk of money."

"I like that rule," Ms. Friendly replied, and winked at Felix.

"And the other rule, we start with dessert." His mom

led Laura Friendly to the counter and offered her a slice of apple or pumpkin pie and a glass of wine.

"This rule is even better." Ms. Friendly took a small slice of each.

After they finished first dessert, Felix helped put the finishing touches on dinner. His mom would not allow their guests in the kitchen. Felix mashed potatoes and set out dishes.

Then they all gathered around their small table with its mismatched chairs. They had so much food that not all of it fit. They rotated platters from the counter to the table and back. Eating and laughing. Felix snuck pieces of turkey to Freebie. And he caught Laura Friendly sharing her roll with the dog too.

After they'd eaten enough for eight people, cleared the table, and loaded the dishwasher, Felix grabbed Freebie's leash.

"Walking the dog? May I join you?" Ms. Friendly asked. "I need some exercise."

"Sure."

They walked behind the apartment buildings to the trail that circled the pond and picnic area.

"Thank you for inviting me," Ms. Friendly said. "This was nice."

"You're welcome. What do you normally do on Thanksgiving?"

She heavy-sighed. "Go to my sister's place. She has a

lovely home in South Carolina, a lovely husband, three lovely kids, and a not-so-lovely cat."

"And she didn't invite you?"

"No, she invited me." She waved the air in front of her face like bugs were swarming. "Without our father around, it's just not the same."

"I've never spent a holiday with my dad."

"I'm sorry to hear that." She blew on her hands. "I was lucky. My father was a big part of my life. He made sure I didn't work through holidays. He'd be my plus-one for events. I could talk to him about anything. And when he passed away a year and a half ago, I wasn't there for him."

Felix stayed quiet, not sure what to say.

"We'd set up hospice care, and they made him comfortable. But I was out of the country for work and didn't make it back in time. I said my final goodbye to him on the phone, but I don't know if he heard me." Laura Friendly shoved her hands deep into her coat pockets. "Fortunately, my sister was there. But if I was granted a do-over—if I could buy a do-over—I'd be there at his side."

"I guess not even billionaires get do-overs."

"Nope." She shook her head.

They walked back in silence. Felix couldn't think of an easy way to bring up the money and the challenge.

When they got inside the apartment, they played Would You Rather . . . , but a Reggie-created philosophy version.

Would you rather be happy or knowledgeable?

*Would you rather love or be loved (assuming you can't
have both)?*

Would you rather a world without hate or a world without lies?

It might have been the worst game ever, and with each
question, Felix could imagine Benji groaning. Then they
played Monopoly, which, surprisingly, Laura Friendly was
terrible at.

"Monopolies are illegal. I don't want to be good at this
game." Then she borrowed five hundred dollars from Felix
so she wouldn't go bankrupt.

After second dessert, Laura Friendly announced that
she had to leave. She needed to be in London the next day.
It wasn't a holiday overseas.

"Thank you again, Karen," Ms. Friendly said to Felix's
mom. "You're a brilliant woman. Everyone should start with
dessert first."

His mom laughed. "Anytime."

Felix walked with Laura Friendly out of the building. He
didn't want to ruin their Thanksgiving, but he had to try to
get her to understand what was happening.

"She quit her job," Felix blurted out.

"Excuse me?" Ms. Friendly stopped walking.

"My mom quit one of her jobs because she thinks I'm a
millionaire," Felix explained. "And we're not going to win
your challenge. We have almost one-point-nine million to

spend, parents breathing down our necks, and we're an internet joke."

She held up a finger. "Your mom said no talking about money." He couldn't tell if she was serious.

"I want to renegotiate," Felix said. "Just let us keep the rest of the money without having to spend it. Benji and I will split it."

Laura Friendly clicked her tongue, and Felix knew the answer before she spoke.

"Is this why you invited me to dinner?"

"No." His voice got lost in his throat. It wasn't the only reason.

She frowned. "Felix, I cannot change the rules."

"Of course you can. Just let us withdraw—"

"Can't be done. I set it up with my lawyers. I made it so no one—myself included—could change the rules. You can spend the money, but you cannot withdraw it and move it to another account."

"We'll buy stock or a house and then sell it—"

"You can't." She shook her head. "You signed a contract. The lawyers will seize all assets you have after December first. Leonard Trulz's job depends on it. He will not be paid if any rules are broken. He has a bonus structure tied to the successful conclusion of this venture."

"What do you mean?"

"If Trulz allows the game to continue after rules have

been broken, he will not be paid a bonus of five hundred thousand dollars." She didn't look proud of this condition. "It's honestly out of my hands."

"Well, then just give us a million dollars," Felix snapped. "You could write a check right now."

Laura Friendly flinched like she'd been hit. "And why would I do that?"

"Because we're friends." Felix stared her in the eyes.

"I don't like your definition of a friend." She ducked into the open town car, and the driver closed the door.

Felix stood in the cold without his jacket. He tried to think of something he could say to Ms. Friendly. Did he owe her an apology? Everything was so messed up. He'd just asked her for a million dollars. *Who does that?* When kids at school asked him to buy them Nintendos or iPhones, it made him feel lousy. They were only interested in his debit card. At times, he was thankful for the no-gift rule. He couldn't buy them things, and that meant he didn't have to wrestle with the decision.

The back window of the car lowered. Felix stepped closer.

"You have almost two million dollars and a week to do whatever you want," she continued.

That's not true.

"Why not enjoy the next few days and the last few dollars? Next Thursday, your life will return to normal. You are

Cinderella at the ball. Stop thinking about what happens after midnight."

The window closed, and the town car drove off.

You're wrong. Felix sat on the curb alone. *My life will never go back to normal.*

Chapter $36

SUNDAY, NOVEMBER 28

Benji

Benji kicked off his hotel slippers, pulled off his shirt, and then cannonballed into the hotel pool. Felix, who'd been floating on his back with his eyes closed, screamed.

"Jerk!" Felix said when he recovered. But his smile gave him away. "When did you get back?"

"An hour ago," Benji said. "I convinced my mom we should stay at the hotel tonight. It's already paid for, and I told her you picked up my homework from last week."

It also helped that Benji had been a perfect kid while the Porters were in Aruba. When his parents had said to eat his vegetables, he'd asked for extra broccoli. When they'd said to turn off the TV, he'd suggested going for a walk. When they'd said time for bed, he'd brushed his teeth and kissed them good night. Not once did he step out of line.

Freebie barked like he was on repeat mode.

"This mutt really wants to doggy-paddle," Reggie said, doing double duty as dog-sitter and Felix's personal lifeguard.

"Let him go," Felix said.

Reggie unclipped the leash. The dog ran, belly-flopped, and swam right to Benji.

"Missed you too, boy." Benji let Freebie kiss his chin, cheek, forehead, and ear. "Okay, okay. Enough of the smooches."

"Hey, bosses." Reggie walked to the edge of the pool. "I'm glad you're both here. We need to talk. Our one-month arrangement is almost up. This has been the best job I've ever had. Much better than the summer I worked at my uncle's funeral home."

Benji shuddered, but it wasn't the thought of dead bodies or the pool temperature that got to him. It was Reggie. They had to fire him.

"That's good, I guess," Felix said as he helped Freebie onto solid ground.

"Yeah, it's been fun. Even if it sometimes feels like *I'm* majoring in philosophy," Benji said.

Reggie snapped his fingers and pointed at Benji. "You got the philosophy lessons for free."

"Gee, thanks."

"But I think it's time I move on," Reggie said. "I need to focus on school and my future."

"You're quitting?" Benji asked.

"I'm giving you my notice." Reggie leaned over and held out his hand to Benji and then to Felix. "You're good bosses. Good men. After December first, you will still be good people. Don't forget that."

Benji nodded. *December first?* They'd never told Reggie about the challenge, but Reggie was a smart guy. He had to know something was up.

Freebie whined and shook, spraying Reggie with water.

"You want me to dry this dog off?" Reggie asked. "While I still work for you?"

"Yes, please," Felix said.

When Benji was certain Reggie had moved out of hearing range, he whispered to Felix. "You're in here doing a back float. Does that mean you've spent all the money? December first is only three days away."

Felix shook his head slowly. "I've been trying. But my mom is watching everything I do. I have to bring my laptop into the bathroom so I can buy stuff online." He sighed. "We still have over one-point-seven million."

"Good," Benji said. "That should just be enough."

"I don't understand." Felix stared at him. "You haven't spent a dime since you've been gone."

"No. My parents cut me off. I didn't have my phone, my iPad, my computer, my debit card. I didn't have anything but television." He wriggled his eyebrows at Felix. "And you can learn a lot from TV. I watched a show about billionaires. There was this Wall Street guy and his supermodel wife. They spent twenty million dollars on their baby's first birthday party."

"Really? How?"

"They had these dolls made to look like their daughter, and every guest got one, like a party favor."

"That sounds creepy."

"It was." Benji shivered, thinking back to the glass-eyed dolls. "They also had Ferris wheels, helicopter rides, and a petting zoo with baby tigers and pandas."

Felix's eyes grew large. If he'd been a cartoon, dollar signs would have danced in his pupils.

"I have a plan. Let's go to my suite. We'll order everything off the room service menu. For old times' sake."

Twenty minutes later, they were in Benji's bedroom, huddled around his computer. His mom was in the living room area, and they couldn't risk her shutting down their final project.

"Whose birthday bash is this going to be?" Felix asked. "We could say it's Freebie's birthday."

"Or we could hijack someone else's event," Benji said.

"Like we hijacked Georgie and Michelle's wedding."

"That was an awesome wedding. If everyone hadn't gotten so worked up about money, it would've been the wedding of the decade." Benji wanted that to be true. It wasn't that *they* had ruined the ceremony or the reception. It was the money that had caused the problem.

Felix shrugged. "I'm sorry about basketball—"

"No!" Benji cut him off. "I know you're good at apologies, but it's not necessary. We're business partners. We need to focus on that, and we need to focus on Alma's drama club fundraiser. That's how we're going to spend the rest of the money."

"But you—"

"No!" Benji did not want to talk about basketball or try-outs or what it felt like to be ignored. That wasn't important. Not now.

Felix sighed. "When is the fundraiser?"

"Wednesday." How did Felix not know? Alma had hung cute signs all over school.

"That's December first," Felix said. They were both very aware of the date.

"Yep, we're finishing this project on the day it's due." Benji smiled.

"And Alma is okay with this?" Felix asked.

"I told her I'd supply the pizza and other food. What's the big deal if we add helicopter rides?" Benji pulled his computer closer. "Once we get everything figured out, I'll tell her." He looked forward to an excuse to talk to her.

"This is our last chance. It has to work." Felix looked less than convinced.

"It will, buddy. And we need to invite Laura Friendly to the fundraiser. Send her a text. I can't wait to see her face when we win."

FELIX: You're invited to the drama club fundraiser

FELIX: Dec 1st—6pm—Stirling Middle School

LAURA FRIENDLY: Wouldn't miss it

Chapter $37

MONDAY, NOVEMBER 29

Felix

Felix woke up before his alarm and before Freebie. The boys finally had a plan to win the challenge.

According to their estimates, by the end of the day on Wednesday, Felix and Benji would be broke. They planned to sink every last penny into the drama club fundraiser: custom cupcakes flown in from a bakery in LA, skywriting, prepaid food trucks, a performance by two Broadway stars, flowers from Holland (which was a six-figure expense!), acrobats, real penguins, and a traveling planetarium. And because Stirling Middle probably wouldn't authorize half of this, they planned to have some of the attractions off school property. But they had a solution for that too: a shuttle service.

They still had dozens of details to figure out, and Benji had to talk to Alma. But Felix was confident it would all come together. It had to.

Felix took a quick shower and put on a pair of tie-dyed leather skater pants that had cost over five grand. He fed and walked Freebie. Then he ate his room service breakfast. By the end of the week, it would be back to off-brand frosted flakes and clothes from Target, and he couldn't wait. He was tying his Air Flights when there was a knock.

Freebie went into ballistic mode, barking and trying to claw through the heavy door.

"Calm down." Felix pulled the dog back and opened the door. It was Georgie.

"Hi," she said.

"You're back." He stated the obvious.

Georgie stepped into the hotel room. Her hair was in a ponytail, and she was dressed for work.

"I brought you this." She handed him a box of maple candy.

"Thanks." He let go of Freebie's collar and took the candy. He and Georgie hadn't seen each other since the wedding. He needed to apologize but didn't know where to start. He'd hoped to have this conversation after December first.

She took a seat at the table and helped herself to a piece of bacon. "I wanted to talk about the wedding."

He let out a breath. "I'm so sorry, Georgie." He collapsed into the chair next to her. "I ruined your wedding. I didn't mean to. I swear."

"Stop." She held up a hand. "I shouldn't have yelled.

You're just a kid. Sometimes I forget that and expect you to act like an adult. That's not fair."

He didn't know what to say. He wasn't *just a kid*.

"You bought me a really stupid wedding gift." She sighed and rolled her eyes. "A really stupid *and* expensive wedding gift. But it was still a gift."

"And it was still stupid," he mumbled, and she laughed.

"I heard Apex-7 returned the money."

"Yeah. Most of it."

"That's good." She paused and stared at him. "Ya know, people say money can change someone, and they don't usually mean for the better."

The pancakes in his stomach churned. *What is she trying to say?*

"But I don't think that's happened to you. You're still a sweet kid, Felix." She got up, and he worried that she might try to kiss his forehead or something. "And if I'm going to be mad about anything, it's not the surprise concert."

"Huh?"

"It's that you wore my wedding dress." She playfully slapped him in the back of the head. "There was a soda stain on the sleeve."

Georgie left, and Felix finished getting ready for school. At seven-thirty, he went to the parking lot.

"Good morning, Reggie." Felix and Freebie crawled into the back of the Range Rover. When the car door opened again, Felix assumed it was Benji.

"Right after basketball practice, we'll go—"

"Excuse me, Mr. Rannells. There's a problem with your account." The hotel manager leaned into the backseat.

"What do you mean?"

"Your rooms are prepaid through December first, but every morning we charge the previous day's incidentals, like room service and pet cleaning fees. Today the payment was denied."

"Oh, sorry." Felix opened the banking app on his cell phone. The balance showed over one million dollars, but there was also a red banner that told him to contact his financial institution. He dialed Mr. Trulz, but the accountant didn't answer. And he always answered.

Felix felt his heartbeat in his temples.

"I'll be right back." He grabbed Freebie's leash and ran to the elevator and rode it to the top floor.

Benji opened the door before Felix could knock. He was dressed for school, but he looked sick.

"What's going on?" Felix asked.

"My dad. His lawyers froze the account. We can't spend any more money until we see a judge on December sixteenth."

Felix's knees buckled, and he crashed butt-first onto the floor. Freebie jumped into his lap, looking for attention.

"You okay?" Benji knelt down next to Felix.

"No." Felix looked up at Benji. *What a stupid question!*

"Don't worry. I'll figure something out." Benji lifted Felix by the elbow and pressed the elevator button. "Just go to school. I'll see you there."

Felix and Freebie went back to the car. The manager still lingered nearby, but Felix ignored him and got into the SUV.

"What's up, boss?" Reggie asked when they were on the road.

"I don't think I'm your boss anymore." Felix stared out the window. "The money is gone."

"Dang, you spent it all?"

"I wish."

Reggie shot him a look in the rearview mirror.

"Benji's parents have control of the money. I can't pay you anymore." Felix's voice shook. "But I'd appreciate it if you dropped me off at school first."

"No problem, Felix, and I can pick you up, too."

"Thank you. And can you still watch Freebie?"

"Happy to."

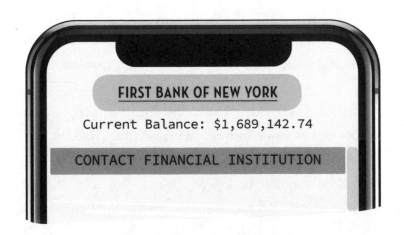

FIRST BANK OF NEW YORK

Current Balance: $1,689,142.74

CONTACT FINANCIAL INSTITUTION

Benji did not deliver on his promise to get the money back. Before every class, Felix checked the app to see if the funds were available. He couldn't concentrate on anything else. Felix asked about it at lunch, and Benji only replied, "Working on it." (This was hard to believe since he was sitting in the cafeteria picking at a turkey sandwich.) When Felix went to basketball, he missed shots, tripped on his own feet, and caught a pass with his face. He had to sit out five minutes until his nose stopped bleeding.

After practice, he grabbed his backpack and jacket and didn't bother to change. There was a text from Benji. Finally!

BENJI: I have a plan.

He has a plan? Felix felt lighter reading those words. Maybe his world wasn't about to fall apart. Felix didn't bother to call or text. He asked Reggie to drive him straight to the Porters' house. Benji was shooting hoops in the driveway under a giant spotlight.

Felix and Freebie got out of the SUV.

"What's going on? Did you talk to your dad?" Felix's breath created a fog in the cold air.

"He won't change his mind." Benji dribbled the ball with two hands. "But I have a plan."

"What?"

"I know my dad's password. We'll log in to his email, and you can write his lawyer a message and tell them to drop the case. Something like: *Objection, I've changed my mind. Please cease and desist. I don't want to sue Laura Friendly anymore. Give them the money back.*"

Felix stared in disbelief. This was not a plan. This was a crappy idea.

"Benji, that's stupid!"

"Hey!" Benji stopped dribbling. "Don't call me stupid."

"Then don't suggest stupid ideas." Freebie pulled on his leash, and Felix snapped it back.

Reggie opened his door and got out of the Range Rover. "Hey! Calm down, guys. Whatever it is, you'll figure this out."

"I can't write an email to a lawyer," Felix continued. "He'd never believe me. And the lawyer would probably call your dad to double-check. It is *stupid.*"

"Then what should we do?" Benji stepped closer, and Freebie jumped up to greet him. The dog didn't realize Benji had screwed up everything and that Freebie would probably be shipped to the animal shelter by the end of the week.

"Tell your dad to release the money!" Felix screamed, and pulled on the leash.

"I can't tell my dad what to do. Can you tell *your* dad what to do?"

"Whoa, Benji, calm down," Reggie said, stepping between them.

The weather was cold enough to snow, but Felix's face was burning hot, and every muscle in his body shook with anger.

"Stop being a useless idiot for once," Felix said through a clenched jaw. "And get the money back!"

"Shut up! And don't call me an idiot!" Benji hurled the ball into the side of the brick house. It sounded like a small explosion.

Felix jumped.

And Freebie darted. His leash snapped from his collar. In a blink, he was across the dark yard and flying toward the main road.

"Freebie!" Felix ran after his dog.

But he was too late. A red truck rounded the corner, and Freebie disappeared beneath it.

Chapter $38

MONDAY, NOVEMBER 29

Benji

Reggie drove through two yellow lights as they raced to the emergency vet. Benji tried to help navigate, keeping his eyes peeled for police cars and other cars in general. He didn't want to look into the backseat. Freebie lay wrapped in a blanket across Felix's lap—motionless.

"Is he still breathing?" Benji asked.

"I don't know," Felix said.

They pulled up outside the pet ER. Two women in scrubs were waiting with a gurney because Reggie had wisely called ahead.

Benji jumped out of the car before it completely stopped, and yanked open the back door for Felix and Freebie.

"Hurry!" He waved the women closer.

They gently lifted Freebie from the backseat and onto the gurney.

"We got him," said the woman with a blond ponytail. "You go in through the main entrance."

"His name is Freebie," Felix said as his injured dog was rushed away.

Reggie, Benji, and Felix followed the sidewalk to the front of the short brick building.

A woman with a sad smile greeted them at the desk. She fiddled with papers on a clipboard. "Has your dog been here before?"

"No," Felix said.

"Please fill out this information, all three sheets. We will also need a five-hundred-dollar deposit." Her voice lowered when she talked about the money.

Felix whipped out his replacement debit card and dropped it on the desk. "Take five thousand. Take it all. I don't care. Just help Freebie."

"We'll do everything we can. Dr. Rhamid is the best." She picked up the card and turned toward her computer.

"It's not going to work," Benji reminded Felix. "The money is not available."

Felix's shoulders fell.

"Here." Reggie pulled out his wallet and fished around for a Visa. "Five hundred, right?"

"We'll pay you back," Benji said to Reggie, who nodded.

Once the money was handled, they took seats in the

hard plastic chairs that made up the waiting room. A TV in the corner was tuned to Animal Planet.

"What home address should I put? The hotel?" Reggie asked, starting on the paperwork.

"Use mine." Benji took the clipboard. When they finished, they gave it back to the receptionist.

"I'll let you know as soon as we have an update." She gave Benji her sad smile again.

Then Benji began making calls—his mom, Ms. Rannells, and finally Alma. He liked having a job, even if it was sharing bad news. Waiting was the worst. He tried to watch the TV. It was better than watching Felix, who had his elbows on his knees and his head in his hands. His body shook as he cried quietly.

Benji's parents showed up thirty minutes later. He hugged his mom. When her arms wrapped around him, his eyes clouded, like he'd been waiting for her shoulder.

He felt a pat on his back from his dad. His mom released her embrace, and he hugged his dad.

"It's going to be all right," his dad said. "We'll get through this." Those few words made them feel like a team again. Something he hadn't felt in a while.

Benji's mom sat next to Felix. She squeezed his hand and whispered something. Felix nodded slightly without looking up.

They settled into the chairs, taking up half the waiting

area. Other people came in with their sick animals—a dog that had swallowed a corncob, a lethargic cat, a puppy that refused to eat. Felix and Benji waited silently.

It felt like a year before the door to the back part of the hospital opened. A short woman in a white lab coat came out. She exchanged a look with the receptionist, who pointed at them.

"I'm Dr. Rhamid. Let's talk in the back."

Felix was the first out of his chair. They all followed Dr. Rhamid into an empty exam room that smelled like ammonia.

"Where's Freebie?" Felix asked.

"They're prepping him for surgery." She clasped her hands and then explained the extent of the injuries: broken bones, punctured lung, internal bleeding, brain swelling.

"But he'll be okay?" Benji interrupted her list of problems.

"I don't know." She shook her head. "We will do all we can, if that's what you want. But you should be prepared for any outcome and difficult decisions."

"Decisions?" Benji asked, but he knew what she was getting at.

"Sometimes the humane thing to do is the hardest. We have to consider the quality of life, including long-term pain and special needs." The doctor looked to the adults in the room.

"We have money!" Felix suddenly shouted. "We can pay anything. Thousands. Millions. Anything! Just save him." Tears streamed down his red cheeks. "Please." His voice cracked.

Technically, they still had $1,689,142.74. They would give every penny of it to save Freebie. And if they won an additional ten million, Benji would give that over too.

"We will do everything we can. But we might not be able to save him." The doctor tilted her head and pushed up her glasses.

Benji swallowed the knot forming in the back of his throat and wiped his eyes on his shirtsleeve.

"We've got millions," Felix repeated. "Take it all."

Dr. Rhamid put a hand on Felix's shoulder. "I'm sorry. It's not about money."

Chapter $39

MONDAY, NOVEMBER 29

Felix

"I'm not going anywhere without my dog," Felix said to his mom.

"You need some sleep. We'll come back in the morning." It was just after 10:00 p.m. Reggie and Mr. and Mrs. Porter had left. Felix's mother had volunteered to stay with the boys. Now, it seemed, she was changing her mind.

"I'm not leaving."

"Okay." She didn't push any more.

Dr. Rhamid had taken Freebie into surgery three hours ago, and there had been no update on the dog's condition, only an update on the medical bill. The total was over three thousand dollars and growing.

His mom leaned her head back against the wall and closed her eyes. Felix was exhausted but not sleepy.

"This is taking too long." Benji ran his hands through his hair.

Felix nodded. He clung to the thought that no news was good news. Freebie was alive. Had to be. If he wasn't, the doctor would have told them.

But the vet could walk through the door at any second and give them the worst news. It made Felix's chest ache.

How much longer?

"I'm sorry, Felix," Benji mumbled. "This is all my fault. All of it. Taking the twenty. The wedding video. My dad shutting down our account. Freebie getting hit." He sniffed, and his shoulders shook. "And emailing Dad's lawyer was a stupid idea. I *am* an idiot. The world's biggest idiot. And now Freebie might . . ."

"You're not an idiot." Felix glanced at Benji. "I shouldn't have said that." Felix had been so mad about the money and the lawyers. But being mad was better than what he was feeling now.

"You were just honest." Benji wiped his nose with the back of his hand.

"I was a jerk. I'm sorry." Felix swallowed. "And we're both to blame for all of this. We're in this mess together."

"We stole money. Maybe we deserve this."

"No. Because Freebie never did anything wrong. He didn't deserve this. That can't be how this—how life— works." Felix didn't care about blame. He didn't care about the money or finding a new apartment or his mom going back to school. That stuff would work out. Somehow. "Freebie didn't deserve this," he repeated.

"Maybe he did," Benji said, and Felix's head snapped up, disgusted. "He chewed up the steering wheel on a Bugatti. That's gotta be bad karma or something."

Felix laughed even though he still felt like his insides were crumbling.

"And he pooped in the elevator once," Felix added. "But that was my fault. I took too long to get my shoes on."

"I think he ate one of the remotes in my suite," Benji said. "And he definitely tried to steal a tooth from the T. rex skull."

They laughed until they were on the edge of tears again.

"I just want him to get better," Felix said.

"That's all I want too." Benji twisted the end of his shirt. "It's funny. You think you want something. Like really want it. Then in an instant, it doesn't matter. I would've given up all our money to make the basketball team. If I made the team . . ." He hesitated. "I'd be good at something."

Felix felt a stab of guilt in his gut. "I'm sorry I ignored you during tryouts."

"It's okay." Benji shrugged. "If I was the good player and you were the one who stunk, I would've ignored you."

"No, you wouldn't have. And it's not okay. We're supposed to be partners. We're supposed to be friends." Felix cleared his throat. He wasn't saying this right. "We *are* friends. With or without the money."

"Well, it looks like we're going to be without."

"I know."

Tuesday, November 30

Dr. Rhamid finally walked into the waiting room just after midnight. Felix searched her expression for some kind of sign.

Is Freebie okay? Is Freebie alive? Is Freebie...

"Would you like to see your dog?" she asked, and that answered one question.

"Yes." Felix nudged his mom awake.

They followed Dr. Rhamid to a room where Freebie lay still on a table. The lights in the room were low, and it felt like they should whisper and tiptoe. A technician stroked Freebie's head gently. Felix stared at Freebie's chest until he saw it rise.

"Is he okay?" Benji asked as they gathered around the dog.

"He's a fighter," Dr. Rhamid said with a half smile. "He had some issues during surgery, but he refused to give up. We will know more after the anesthesia wears off and in the coming days. If he does well, he'll need another surgery for his leg."

If he does well? Felix refused to consider the *if.*

"You should go home," the doctor continued. "We will call you immediately with any updates."

Felix leaned his nose against Freebie's. It felt dry when it should have been wet. And Freebie should have licked Felix's face and wagged his tail.

"I love you, boy," Felix whispered. "And we'll take care of you. No matter what."

"Just get better. Please," Benji mumbled into Freebie's bandaged ear.

Felix's mom placed a hand on Felix's back and rubbed a small circle. She used to do this when he had nightmares.

"Let's go home," she said.

They walked to the front of the building. When they reached the outside door, the guy at the desk stopped them.

"Excuse me. I'm sorry. We need you to take care of your dog's bill."

"Right now?" Felix's mom asked.

"It's our policy. Sadly, sometimes owners don't return for their pets." He held out a sheet of paper.

"That won't happen with us." Felix couldn't imagine people abandoning their dogs.

The back door opened, and Dr. Rhamid walked into the lobby. Felix worried she was going to deliver bad news, but she smiled and tapped her empty mug before heading to the coffee machine in the corner.

Felix's mother grabbed the bill, and he looked over her shoulder. His eyes immediately found the total—$3,819.04. Yesterday, that amount would've been no problem.

"I can't pay that," his mom said.

"I'm sorry, ma'am. We require full payment, or we cannot treat your dog."

"What? You can't do that!" Felix balled his fists.

Benji stepped up to the desk. "We'll pay it. We'll pay it. Tomorrow." Then he patted his pockets. "I just forgot my wallet."

"If you're worried about us not coming back, then we just won't leave," Felix said. "I'll stay here until Freebie is better." He sat in one of the plastic chairs, ready to stay for days if he had to.

Dr. Rhamid stepped forward. "It's okay, Andy. Let them take care of the bill another day. It's very late."

The receptionist gave a slight nod. "I'll put a note on your account."

Benji had to practically drag Felix out of the animal hospital. An inch of snow had fallen. Benji offered to scrape the car, but Felix's mom refused the help. The boys climbed into the backseat while she cleared the windows.

"What are we going to do?" Felix asked. "We need to pay Freebie's bills." Money alone wouldn't save Freebie. But without it, Freebie had no chance.

"I might know a way to get the money back," Benji

whispered. "It would be bending the rules, but not exactly breaking them."

"How? What do you mean?"

"I know how to tell my parents without really *telling* them. If they know the truth about the challenge, I bet they'll drop the lawsuit and release the money."

"Do it!"

Felix didn't care if it was bending—or breaking—the rules. He didn't care if they won or lost. He only cared about Freebie.

Chapter $40

TUESDAY, NOVEMBER 30

Benji

Benji stood in his room that morning. He'd only slept a few hours, and his eyes felt heavy and his brain sluggish. But he had to tell his parents about the challenge without really telling them. He pulled out his iPad and started a new entry.

November 30

I'm not always honest when I write in here. I want to sound like the good guy. Somebody who wins stuff and who people like. Someone who would make his parents proud. But here's the truth. The last twenty-four hours have been the hardest of my life. Freebie was hit by a car and almost died. He still might not make it. And I fought with my best friend over money.

See, Laura Friendly didn't just give Felix and me five million dollars. It was a challenge. We had to spend it all in thirty days, and then we'd get an actual reward. And we couldn't tell anyone. That was part of the rules. We have until the end of the day tomorrow to spend the last of it. If we do, I'll win ten million. If we don't, that's it. Game over.

But my parents' lawyers have locked up all the money. It might as well be in Gringotts because I can't get to it. Felix and I can't win unless we spend it. And we can't pay Freebie's vet bills. That dog means everything to Felix and to me.

I didn't make the basketball team. I'm not a good student. It would have been awesome to come home with a giant check for ten million dollars. That would have made my parents proud. Maybe someday, I'll be more than a screw-up.

Over and out,
Benji

He turned off his iPad and left for school.

• • •

Benji sat at an empty table near the trash cans. He'd forgotten his lunch, but he didn't have an appetite anyway.

"Can I join you?"

He looked up to see Alma smiling at him.

"Sure."

She sat across from him. "How's your dog?" He liked that she said "your dog." Freebie might have spent more time with Felix, but Benji loved that stupid mutt just as much. He was sure of it.

"Same."

"No lunch?" she asked.

He shook his head.

"Want some of mine?" She held up half of a wrap. "It's not as good as pizza."

"Thanks." He grinned. "Alma, I'm really sorry about the drama club fundraiser. I was planning all sorts of amazing things . . . and now everything is a mess. The money is gone, and Freebie is . . ." He almost said "dying" but caught himself. "Freebie's not okay."

"Don't worry about the fundraiser." She touched his hand for a second. "I don't know what you were planning. But it's fine."

"There were penguins," he mumbled.

She laughed. "What? You get Apex-7 for the wedding, but I get penguins? I've been to the aquarium. Penguins reek like rotten fish. No, thank you."

Benji tapped his forehead. "Note to self, Alma doesn't like penguins."

She laughed again. "You'll still come, right? There are no penguins, but we're having craft vendors, a magician, and an auction. You can bid on a gift basket from Sprinkles."

"That's *our* place." He hadn't meant to say that. His cheeks burned.

"It is," she said, and he instantly felt better.

"I'll be there."

● ● ●

When Benji walked into the kitchen after school, his mom was sitting at the counter with her hands wrapped around a coffee mug. The moment her eyes flicked to him, she was out of her seat and wrapping him in a hug. He knew she'd listened to the journal entry.

"I'm proud of you, Benji. Every day. I'm proud of you." Her voice quivered, and he thought she might be crying, but she held him so tight that he couldn't see her face.

"For what?"

"You are my son, and I'll love you no matter what."

"Love is not the same as being proud," he mumbled.

She stepped back to look him in the eyes. "You are a good kid, Benji, with the biggest heart. I think that's more important than grades or basketball. Don't you?"

"I guess," he said.

"I love you so much."

"I know," Benji said.

"Do you? Because if you don't, that's my failure." She touched her heart. "This is not something that has to be earned."

She squeezed him again, and then Benji heard someone clearing their throat. His dad stood in the doorway leading to the dining room.

His father and mother exchanged a look, and she made an excuse about needing to check an email and left them alone.

Benji took a seat at the table. He didn't want to start the conversation because he didn't know how.

"We've dropped the lawsuit," his dad said.

"Thank you." He let out a deep breath. They could help Freebie now.

"I wish you'd talked to us sooner."

Benji ran his finger over the spot in the table where he'd etched his name in the wood with a fork years ago. He'd ruined the furniture like he ruined everything else.

"I couldn't," he said.

"I'm not talking about the money." His dad sat across the table and didn't speak again until Benji met his eyes. "Benji, I don't care if you don't play basketball. I don't care if you don't get As, as long as you put in the effort."

"I think every parent says that, and I don't think any kid

has ever believed it." Benji shook his head. "If I have a kid someday, I'll never say, 'It's okay if you don't do good, as long as you try hard.'"

His dad leaned back in the chair. "Then what *will* you say to your kid?"

"Son." Benji stuck out his chest and used his deepest voice. "I want perfect test scores and first-place trophies. You should be good at music, playing trumpet solos at concerts and stuff. You should score the most points on your basketball team, your baseball team, your soccer team, your cricket team."

"Cricket?" His dad chuckled. "What do you know about cricket?"

"I know my son will be the best at it."

"And if he's not?" his dad asked.

"Then he's not good enough to be a Porter." Benji was trying to be funny. But watching the sadness move across his dad's eyes, he knew it wasn't.

His father didn't speak for what felt like an hour. Benji fidgeted in his seat, waiting.

"You and your mother are the most important things to me," his dad finally said. "And nothing you do or don't do could change how I feel about you."

Benji knew this—or had known this at one time. But to hear his dad say it now, he almost felt silly for ever doubting it.

"You are a Porter and my son. You are more than enough." Benji's dad took a breath. "And I'm sorry if I ever made you doubt that."

Benji sniffed hard. The tightness in his throat made it hard to speak, so he just nodded.

Chapter $41

WEDNESDAY, DECEMBER 1

Felix

Felix walked into the gym for the drama club fundraiser. The room was crowded with tables hosted by people selling hand-knitted hats, Christmas wreaths, and shirts with vinyl lettering that said things like DRAMA MAMA and WORLD'S BEST GRANDMA.

He didn't want to be there. He wanted to be at the vet hospital with Freebie. This morning, he'd paid off Freebie's ever-growing bill of $4,991.00 and asked the receptionist to take another fifty thousand for Freebie's future needs. She had refused to charge that much but did take another five hundred as a deposit.

It probably wouldn't be enough.

Felix spotted Benji working at the bake sale, wearing a cotton-candy-pink apron. Benji had begged him to come.

"Hey, Felix. What can I get you? A brownie? A cookie? Cake square?"

283

FIRST BANK OF NEW YORK

Current Balance: $1,641,512.58

RECENT TRANSACTIONS

Dec 1, Cherry Street Animal Hospital (Freebie–Deposit)
                                                    –$500.00

Dec 1, Cherry Street Animal Hospital
(Freebie–Balance)   –$4,991.00

Dec 1, To: Reggie Fazil (Payroll–Back Pay) –$39,449.16

Dec 1, The Grand Regency (Incidentals)   –$2,690.00

"Why are we here?" Felix asked.

"I've found a way to spend the rest of the money." Benji wriggled his eyebrows.

"We can't win," Felix sighed. "We broke a rule."

"We bent a rule."

"We still have over one-point-six million left."

"And we're not giving up until the final buzzer." Benji rubbed his palms together. "This is our buzzer-beater moment."

"Are you going to charge me a million dollars for a cupcake?"

"Nope." Benji looked at his phone. "I've got something better. And it's about to start." He took off his apron, moved closer to the stage, and waved for Felix to follow.

Alma stood behind a podium and adjusted the microphone. She thanked everyone for attending and then read off the winners of the silent auctions. The prizes included VIP seating for *Shrek,* signed books, tee times, and about a thousand different gift baskets. She never once mentioned Benji's name.

"What's going on?" Felix whispered to Benji.

"Just wait."

"And we have one final item," Alma said. "Mr. Palomino will tell you about it." She stepped aside and, as she did, gave a little wave in Benji's direction.

The principal took over the microphone. "Our last auction item is not the silent type. We will be bidding live. At stake is your principal as your personal assistant for one day. I will carry bags, attend classes, do homework, serve a four-course lunch. Your wish is my command. Within reason, of course."

"This is it," Benji said.

"We'll start the bidding at twenty-five dollars." The principal scanned the crowd.

"Twenty-five." A tall man standing next to his tall daughter held up his hand.

Then Benji stepped forward. "I bid $1,641,512.58!"

No one had expected that, including Felix. He felt a surge of confusion and excitement, and maybe even hope.

Could we really spend all the money on this? Could we win?

"Benji Porter, that's not appropriate." Mr. Palomino pointed at him.

Benji held his hands out wide. "Am I not allowed to bid?"

"Keep it reasonable, or I'll ask you to leave." Mr. Palomino looked to the audience. "Do I hear forty dollars?"

Benji's cheeks turned red.

Someone in the back of the room shouted "Forty!"

"Do I hear sixty dollars?" the principal asked.

"Sixty." Benji raised his arm. "Am I allowed to bid sixty?"

The principal nodded slightly but gave his sternest look before asking for one hundred dollars.

The bidding continued between Benji and the rest of the audience, while Felix made his way to the edge of the gym. The challenge was over. He'd accepted that, even if Benji couldn't.

"Benji Porter has bid six hundred dollars," the principal said. "Do I hear six hundred fifty dollars?"

The room fell silent.

"Can I bid a million now?" Benji asked.

"No." Mr. Palomino held up a wooden mallet. "Six hundred going once."

The crowd remained quiet. What did Benji expect? No one else had his kind of money.

"Six hundred going twice." The principal raised his hammer.

No one but Benji had one-point-six million burning a hole in his pocket.

"Six hundred going . . ."

No one but Benji—

And Felix!

"Six hundred and fifty!" Felix yelled.

Every head turned in his direction, but Felix looked only at his partner. Benji's face squished into confusion for half a second and then lit up with understanding.

"Seven hundred!" Benji yelled.

"One thousand." Felix walked to the front of the gym, and the crowd parted to make way. Benji and Felix stood in front of the podium and bid over and over again.

"One hundred thousand!" Benji said.

"Two hundred thousand," Felix countered.

The principal tried to stop them. "Boys! Enough." He pounded his hammer, and Felix didn't know if that meant it was over or if it was just a way to get their attention.

People held out their cell phones and recorded the

event. Felix knew there would be a backlash tomorrow. Another viral video—and he didn't care.

"Five hundred thousand," Felix said.

"Six."

"Seven."

"Eight."

"Nine."

Benji turned and looked straight at Principal Palomino. "$1,641,512.58."

The room fell quiet again.

"Are you done?" the principal asked.

Felix smiled and shrugged. "Yeah, I'm out of money."

And Mr. Palomino looked out of patience. It was obvious that he didn't believe this was real.

"I want to talk to you both after this." Mr. Palomino raised the hammer. "Going once. Going twice. And—"

"Two million!" A voice rang out from the back corner. Felix recognized it without looking.

Laura Friendly.

Chapter $42

WEDNESDAY, DECEMBER 1

Benji

The crowd roared as the gavel cracked against the podium.

Benji couldn't see Laura Friendly, but he knew her voice. She had outbid them. His shoulders tightened, and his hands curled into fists. What was she doing here? Why did she outbid them?

Because she's an evil monster!

Alma was suddenly at his side. She touched his arm, and his rage partially evaporated.

"This is amazing," she said. "We can afford wireless mics that work, cushions for the seats, or maybe a whole new auditorium."

He tried to smile.

"Was this planned?" Alma pointed toward the crowd, where Laura Friendly was lost in the center.

"Absolutely not." Benji exchanged a look with Felix. He didn't seem to know what to make of this either.

"Anyway, thank you." Alma squeezed his arm again.

The principal left the stage and joined them. He put one arm on Benji's shoulder and one arm on Felix's. Benji immediately stepped out of his grasp.

"You had me going there for a minute." Mr. Palomino laughed and shook his head. "Ms. Friendly has been very generous to this school. I need to thank her." Then he made his way through the crowd.

"What just happened?" Benji asked Felix.

"I don't know." Felix shrugged. "Why would she do that?"

"She's a bored billionaire who enjoys torturing kids."

But why does she want us to fail? Other than the obvious reason of not wanting to give away twenty million dollars. Would she even notice if someone took twenty million out of her billions? She'd certainly noticed when they'd taken twenty dollars.

Benji pushed through the people. Laura Friendly, her assistant, *and* the troll stood near a table of auction items. Tracey kept telling everyone no selfies. No questions. But plenty of people took pictures. Mr. Palomino shook Laura Friendly's hand.

Felix snuck in and politely asked, "Can we talk to you, please?"

She nodded and turned toward the door.

"No!" Benji yelled loudly enough to stun the crowd quiet. "We're talking here. Now!"

"Fine," Laura Friendly said, crossing her arms.

"Why are you here? Why did you outbid us?" Benji asked.

"You invited me. Don't you recall?" Laura Friendly said, and they had. On Sunday, which felt like a lifetime ago, they had thought she'd be handing them each a giant check.

"Why outbid us? You made us lose," Benji said.

"Did *I* cause you to lose?" She pulled off her glasses like it might make the lasers shooting from her eyes more effective. "Two days ago, your parents managed to tie up the money with legal proceedings, ultimately ending any hopes you had of spending the final sum. Then Leonard called me this morning." She glanced at the troll. "It seems, with mere hours left in the challenge, the court case was conveniently dismissed, and you were free to spend the money again. The timing felt motivated."

Technically, Benji had never said a word about the challenge to *anyone*. He could deny telling his parents. She didn't have any proof, just a very accurate suspicion.

"What is going on?" Mr. Palomino asked. Their conversation was causing confusion in the crowd.

"What if"—Laura Friendly tapped a finger on her chin—"I offered a million dollars, right now, to anyone in this room who could prove you broke my rules?"

"Oh God!" Tracey said, and then she swore under her breath. "Laura, you have to stop doing this."

Everyone in the room began talking at once. The crowd pushed closer, and Benji thought they might be crushed.

"Stop it! Stop it!" he yelled, and then he said to Laura Friendly, "You're right. It was convenient because my parents found out the truth. They listened to my journal, which I knew they would. It was the only way to get the money back, and we needed it."

"What in heavens for? Another drone? New tennis shoes, perhaps?" Laura Friendly narrowed her eyes.

"For Freebie," Felix said. "He was hit by a car, and we needed to pay his vet bill."

"That's awful." Her face softened. "I'm sorry. Is he okay?"

"No, he's not," Felix said. "We had to bend your rules to help save his life."

"And it was a stupid rule." Benji didn't care if he offended Laura Friendly. "If any rules are meant to be broken, it's the stupid ones."

"Benji," the troll interrupted. "Regardless of how you feel about the rules, with this breach of contract, the challenge is terminated immediately."

Benji didn't know if he should feel relief or disappointment or anger. He just knew he was tired of all of it.

"You're right," Laura Friendly said. "The whole thing was stupid."

"Okay." The principal held up his hands like a fight was about to start. "Someone needs to explain what is happening. What rules? What contract? I don't like the sound of any of this."

"That's exactly what I want to know." Ms. Rannells stood at the edge of the crowd.

"Mom!" Felix said.

But Ms. Rannells just held her hand up to Felix; she was focused on Laura Friendly.

"At this time, Laura Friendly is not making a public statement," Tracey said. "Our office will address the issue as necessary later this week."

"Oh, Tracey, please. I can address this. I took a well-orchestrated publicity opportunity and turned it into an impossible challenge." Laura Friendly shrugged. "It was a mistake."

Benji nodded. Laura Friendly had made a mistake with the challenge. Felix and Benji had made a mistake in accepting it. And it all had started because he'd borrowed twenty dollars.

No, he'd *stolen* twenty dollars.

Benji knew what he had to do. As the principal and others badgered Laura Friendly with questions, Benji made his way to the podium. There was something that had to be said, and he should have said it thirty days ago.

"Excuse me! Excuse me!" He spoke into the microphone. "I feel like I need to explain some things. Last month, on the field trip, Felix and I found Ms. Friendly's wallet."

People nodded because everyone knew this part.

"And we turned the wallet in to the police." Benji

swallowed. "But not before we took twenty dollars. When we realized it was Laura Friendly's wallet, we thought, *What's the big deal? She won't miss it.* So we stole her money to buy hot dogs and ice cream."

Laura Friendly stared at him. He couldn't tell if she wanted him to continue or to shut up. Then she gave the slightest nod.

"Ms. Friendly knew we took her money and didn't deserve a reward." He let out a deep breath. "So she offered us a challenge to spend over five million dollars in a month, but we couldn't tell anyone, and there were about a hundred other rules." Benji exaggerated.

A murmur swept across the room.

Why would you do that?

What were the rules?

Do the parents know?

"We took the challenge, and we failed," Benji admitted. "It's a lot harder than you think. Plus, I'm breaking the rules right now by telling all of you." No way to call *this* a bending of the rules.

Benji glanced at Felix, who was chewing on his thumbnail. A month ago, Benji wouldn't have been able to guess what Felix was thinking. Now he knew his friend was worried about his future.

"I realized something just ten seconds ago," Benji continued. "I never apologized for taking the twenty. I only made excuses." He looked over at Laura Friendly, ignoring everyone else in the room. "I'm sorry, Ms. Friendly. I stole from you, and I'm sorry it took a month to say I'm sorry."

Laura Friendly smiled and mouthed, "Thank you."

"Anyway, feel free to post your videos and make fun of me. But now you know the truth. At least our school is getting a couple million out of this." Benji saluted his audience and then jumped down from the stage.

Laura Friendly didn't answer anyone's questions or make any more statements. Tracey managed to escort her, Felix, Ms. Rannells, and Benji through the crowd and out of the gym. They stood in the hallway near the boys' locker rooms. Benji would have been lying if he'd said he didn't still hope Laura Friendly would change her mind about the money. Maybe say, *I appreciate your apology. Here's ten million dollars.*

But she didn't.

"Guess it's my turn. I owe you both an apology for issuing the challenge. It is not my place to teach you a lesson."

"What is *wrong* with you?" Ms. Rannells didn't seem to be in the mood for apologies. "You gave two twelve-year-old boys a five-million-dollar secret?"

Laura Friendly pushed a strand of hair behind her ear. "When you say it like that, it sounds awful."

"It is awful."

"You're right. I'm sorry. I don't expect I'll be getting an invitation to Thanksgiving next year."

"Oh my God." Ms. Rannells literally shook her fists at

the woman. "I need a minute to think. I need some air." She walked toward the exit.

"Mom?" Felix ran after her.

"I still don't understand," Benji said. "You outbid us because you knew we lost?"

"You had a brilliant idea, bidding against each other in the auction. You were very close to winning."

"Don't remind me," Benji mumbled.

Laura Friendly straightened her coat. "But honestly, I didn't do it to make you lose. I just got caught up in the excitement of the bidding."

Benji rolled his eyes.

"So, what did I win?"

"Basically, a date with our principal." Benji laughed. It was Laura Friendly's turn for torture.

"That sounds horrendous."

"At least you won something." He shoved his hands into his pockets and stuck out his bottom lip.

"Oh, stop your whining." She pretended to shoo him away. "If I just gave you a million dollars, you wouldn't appreciate it when you actually *earned* your first million. I'm doing you a favor."

"That's some nutty billionaire logic. I'm pretty sure I'll always appreciate a million dollars." But he did like the idea that she thought he'd someday be financially successful.

She scoffed. "But maybe you've earned something."

She tapped a finger on her chin, and Benji held his breath. "How about this? You and Felix can each keep one thing you bought. Just one thing. And it can't be a car. Those were rentals."

"Seriously?" Benji didn't know if he should cheer or complain. Laura Friendly was an expert at delivering good news with a disappointing twist.

"Yes, seriously. But whatever you select, you can't sell it. You gotta keep it. Maybe there should be some other rules too."

"No. That's enough."

Chapter $43

WEDNESDAY, DECEMBER 1

Felix

"I knew something was going on, but I never imagined something like this," Felix's mom said. They sat on a buddy bench outside, near the bus parking lot.

Felix was freezing, but his mom didn't seem to notice the temperature.

"I'm sorry I didn't win the money." Felix pulled his knees to his chest. "If I'd won the challenge ... we'd be okay."

"Felix. We are okay." She rubbed the back of her neck and took a breath before continuing. "What did I tell you? You don't need to worry about money. That's not your responsibility. It's mine."

"We don't have an apartment. You quit your job at the warehouse. And I could have made everything better for us." His nose ran—maybe from the cold, possibly from the realization that the challenge was actually over, and they'd lost.

She put an arm around his shoulder. "Hey, hey. I'll figure it out. That is my role as your mom, Felix. I take care of you. You don't take care of me."

"No." He shook his head. "That's not true. We take care of each other."

"Yes. We're a team. But I'm the coach and four of the starting players."

"And what am I?" Felix asked.

"You're the star of the team. You're responsible for playing your best at every game and at every practice. You show up, ready to win but knowing we'll lose sometimes. And you do not need to worry about where we play or where I'm getting the uniforms from."

He glanced at her. "I think that's the manager's job, not the coach's."

"Oh yeah, is that so? Then I'm the manager, too. I'm a busy woman."

He laughed, and his teeth chattered.

"I've done a good job up to this point. Haven't I?" his mom asked.

"Yeah. But you have to admit, ten million would have made your job easier."

"Absolutely. Just like ten thousand made my life easier."

"Ten thousand?" he asked, and it dawned on him as the words left his mouth—*the half-court shot.*

"I'm still working at the nursing home, and that money will help with school and an apartment and even buy

Freebie a few Milk-Bones. And when that's gone, we'll sue Laura Friendly for child endangerment."

"Seriously?" he asked.

"No."

"Can I get new sneakers?" The red-and-white Flights he was wearing were going to *disappear* at midnight.

"Not those Nikes." She patted his shoes. "Those are way too expensive."

Thursday, December 2

In the morning, Felix walked into Stirling Middle School no longer a millionaire, or even a potential millionaire—just an average seventh-grade student. Well, one who'd, yet again, been the star of a viral video. As he made his way down the hall, every head turned, and every conversation paused. He still didn't enjoy the attention, but it didn't bother him as much anymore. Then he spotted Benji waiting for him by his locker, holding a bag from Downtown Donuts.

School was different than it was a month ago. School was better.

"Here ya go. Georgie even gave me a discount." He handed it to Felix.

"Thanks." Felix put his coat and lunch away.

"So did you decide?" Benji asked. "What's the one thing you're going to keep?" Benji had texted the details of the consolation prize last night.

"I don't know. Either my Air Flights or my iPhone." Felix patted his pocket. He really didn't want to give up his phone. He might never get another one. But the sneakers were his favorite shoes ever—and he considered them lucky. "What about you?"

"The Obi-Wan robe."

"Even though it's from *Phantom Menace*?" Felix raised his eyebrows.

"Good point. Maybe the Hermès bag."

Felix closed his locker and turned to go to homeroom—and came face to face with Aidan.

"Look! It's the world's biggest morons." Aidan spoke loudly enough to get everyone's attention. "You seriously couldn't find a way to spend five million in a month? I could do it in a week."

"There were a lot of rules." Benji shrugged and walked between Aidan and Felix.

Aidan scrambled to get in front of Benji. "I'd have bought a mansion."

"No real estate," Benji said as he tried to step around him.

"I'd have taken a cruise around the world." Aidan blocked his path.

"Um, school. Duh? Didn't have time." Benji shook his head.

"Then I'd have bought the Mets," Aidan said.

Benji rolled his eyes and then shared a look with Felix. Neither of them bothered to point out that baseball teams cost way more than five million dollars. (Five million couldn't even buy you a decent relief pitcher.)

"How did you blow this, Felix?" Since Benji didn't seem to be taking the bait, Aidan turned his attacks on Felix. "You're a puny loser, but people say you're smart. Or at least have more brain cells than the giant."

Felix noticed Benji's hands balled into fists. The school had a zero-tolerance policy on violence. If Benji threw a punch—no matter how much Aidan deserved it—he'd be suspended, at the very least. And Aidan would definitely have a dented face.

"Do you know what I think?" Aidan continued. "You two—"

"Do you know what *I* think?" Felix cut Aidan off. "I think I finally get the quote by the philosopher David Hume. The one about the oyster. Remember that one, Benji?"

"Yeah." Benji gave a thoughtful nod. "Let me try to explain it to you, Aidan. In this great big ole universe, man is no more important than an oyster. Or something like that." Benji shrugged, and Felix agreed that it was close enough.

Aidan's face wrinkled. He obviously didn't get it.

"And you, Aidan, are an oyster," Felix explained. "You're just not that important."

"Definitely an oyster," Benji said, and laughed.

"And you're both idiots!" Aidan yelled. "Especially you, *Barney*. You've always been an idiot."

Benji stopped laughing. He took a giant step forward and stood chest to chest with Aidan.

"My name is Benji. Not Barney. Benji." He didn't move, almost daring Aidan to call him anything other than his name.

"Whatever, Bar . . ." Aidan couldn't seem to finish any name. "I'm not an oyster." Then he slunk away.

"I'm not an oyster." Benji did his best Aidan impression.

Both Benji and Felix laughed again. It took a few more minutes before they stopped cracking up and walked toward their homeroom.

"Ya know," Benji said, "to be honest, I still don't think I really understand that Hume quote. We can't *all* be oysters."

"You're not an oyster, buddy."

Ms. Chenoweth stood outside her classroom door as if she'd been waiting for them. "I can't believe that woman gave you such an irresponsible challenge. I'm sorry. Some adults don't think of their influence on children."

"It's not like she locked us in a cage," Benji said.

"We had some fun," Felix added.

"I'm sure you did." Ms. Chenoweth nodded. "I would have taken a nice vacation. Somewhere I could drink out of a coconut by a pool."

"That sounds okay," Benji said. "But also a little boring."

Students gathered.

"You know what I would do?" Madisyn asked. "I'd buy my mom a new car, and then I'd donate the rest. And maybe go to a Clean Cut concert." She pointed to her giant pin of the four-member boy band.

Alma came up behind them and poked Benji in the side. "I'd buy the whole school pizza."

"Very funny." Benji smiled at her, and his face turned pink.

"I'd go to China," Max Wade said, "and see the Great Wall. Maybe buy a Dodge Tomahawk V10 Superbike. It's the coolest motorcycle ever."

Felix shook his head. "There were rules. No vehicles. No charities. No donations. No gifts."

Still, everyone had ideas. Clothes, vacations, plastic surgery, telescopes, traveling circuses, radioactive spiders, trips to the moon, and then the suggestions got weird.

And it gave Felix an idea.

Chapter $44

WEDNESDAY, JANUARY 12

Felix and Benji

Felix intercepted the pass and dribbled down the court. He crossed the ball between his legs, causing one defender to slip. Another chased him. He pulled up at the foul line.

"Shoot!" Benji screamed from the bleachers, spit flying from his mouth. "Shoot!"

In one swift motion, Felix lifted the ball above his head and launched it at the basket.

All net!

"Yes!" Benji yelled. He turned and high-fived Laura Friendly.

"That's thirteen points," she said. "This is his best game yet." She wore the Stirling Middle School sweatshirt Benji had given her at the first game.

"Go, Felix," Reggie said with little enthusiasm, and his face was in a book. Benji didn't understand why Reggie attended games when he didn't seem interested at all. ("I'm a Felix fan, not a basketball fan," Reggie had explained previously.)

Even when the Stirling Wildcats were up by twelve with two minutes left, Felix's cheering section still yelled and clapped for every basket. Benji was the loudest, but Georgie was a close second place.

After the game, Benji suggested they all go for pizza to celebrate the victory. He didn't say who would pay. But Laura Friendly had to leave for DC. Georgie and Michelle were meeting friends. Felix's mom had a class. That left only Reggie, who offered to drive the boys—in his *new* Volkswagen—no charge. (He'd spent some of his earnings to buy a new-to-him used car.)

Benji rode shotgun, and Felix rode in the back. Almost felt like old times, except they were missing Freebie.

"Where's your phone?" Benji asked Felix. "Ms. Friendly sent us the prototype for our game."

"Cool." Felix fished through his duffel bag to find his iPhone. That was the one thing he had decided to keep. The rest of the stuff they'd bought in November had been confiscated by Laura Friendly's goons. Turned out they weren't really goons—just a moving company with a meticulous checklist of all the stuff Benji and Felix had bought.

Felix clicked download, and a few seconds later, a giant dollar sign spun on the screen with the words *Penny Doubled Challenge* pulsing beneath. The game had been Felix's idea, and he'd shared it with Benji first. Then they'd pitched the idea to Laura Friendly together. After all, they had lived it. She liked the concept and offered them a penny for every download. They didn't expect to get rich from it. According to their Google research, most apps never made any money, and a successful one might only make five grand. (Not enough to even buy Frodo's pants.) But the ultra-successful ones could earn fifty million. That would be awesome, even if their parents were making them put all their earnings into college savings accounts.

Once loaded, the *Penny Doubled Challenge* required a player name, and then the user needed to select their rules.

"That's not fair. We didn't get to pick our rules," Benji said.

"We also *really* got five million dollars." Felix shuddered like he couldn't believe it.

Benji laughed. "If we had to do it over again, what would we do differently?"

"Other than *not* take the twenty?" Felix asked.

"Then none of it would have happened. Right, Reggie?" Benji asked. "The ends justify the means."

Reggie sighed. "The ends justifying the means is something a ruthless dictator might say, not a philosopher."

"Really?" Benji asked. "I thought it sounded philosophical."

"Well, some attribute the phrase to Machiavelli in his work *The Prince,* but he never used—"

"Never mind!" Benji laughed. "I take it back."

Felix shook his head. "If we hadn't taken the challenge, we might not have met Reggie. Or adopted Freebie. And Georgie and Michelle might not be married—at least not yet."

"You wouldn't have your lucky sneakers." Benji pointed at the red-and-white Nike Air Flights that Felix wore. They still looked new because Felix cleaned them every night.

The Flights were the one thing Benji had kept. He'd thought about hanging on to the fossils, the comic books, or Obi-Wan's robe. They were all cool. But none of that stuff had meant as much to him as the sneakers meant to Felix.

Felix ran a finger over the swoosh. "They're the reason we're undefeated so far."

"It's almost like it's good that we stole." Benji laughed again.

"Yeah, almost."

"Do you think if we hadn't had this challenge, we'd have become friends?" Benji asked. "We're not in the same classes. I'm not on the basketball team."

"Yes," Felix said quickly, and Benji was surprised at how happy that made him feel. "One way or another, we would have become friends. Fate. That's the right word, isn't it?"

"Yes, fate," Reggie said. "Regardless of the path, it was meant to happen."

"Now, is fate responsible for making you Alma's boyfriend? That I don't know." Felix wriggled his eyebrows at Benji.

"I'm not her boyfriend." Benji's cheeks flushed. He put his palms to his face to try to cool himself off.

"You're Shrek. She's Fiona." Felix snorted.

"Only onstage. That has nothing to do with real life." But Benji hoped Felix was right. He liked Alma a lot, and he liked theater. (Who knew!) And he liked that he could be honest with his parents. But, to be *honest,* he would have liked ten million dollars, too.

Felix would have liked the ten million dollars as well. And it would have changed his life more than Benji's. His mom still worked at the nursing home, and she was going to school at night. They'd moved apartments. The new place had been built in the 1970s, and nothing had been updated since then. His bedroom—he finally had his own room!—was about the size of a closet in Benji's house, but Felix never complained, because the landlord allowed pets. Felix had his own bed (well, he shared it with a dog), and they had a yard.

Freebie had made a complete recovery, except he limped sometimes and was afraid of cars. That was probably a good thing. Laura Friendly had set up a Freebie account for anything the dog needed, from vet appointments to food to chew toys. The troll managed Freebie's account, and he was basically never allowed to say no to any Freebie-related request. Freebie would always be financially cared for by Laura Friendly and physically cared for by Felix (and Benji).

Reggie pulled up to a stoplight. In the lane next to them, a bright blue van idled. On the side was written HOT DIGGITY DOG.

"Hey, look." Benji knocked Felix in the chest. "A food truck. Want a hot dog?"

Felix dramatically patted his pockets. "I don't seem to have any money." He laughed.

"I'm broke too. Feels good to say that."

Benji and Felix knew they both had more than they'd had two months ago. Maybe not a huge bank account, vintage Jordans, a rented Bugatti, and dinosaur fossils. They didn't really want those things anyway—okay, except maybe the car, and classic sneakers were pretty awesome. But now they had a dog, an app that could potentially make millions (hey, a kid can dream), and a guaranteed *buddy* for field trips.

A Penny Doubled

Would you rather have a million dollars now or a penny doubled every day for a month? If you want the higher amount and are willing to wait, take the penny doubled. That's the power of exponential growth.

A quick review of exponents. Here, x is the exponent.

N^x

If we plug in $N = 2$ and $x = 1$, then

$N^x = 2^1 = 2$

If we plug in $N = 2$ and $x = 2$, then

$N^x = 2^2 = (2)(2) = 4$

My favorite way to represent multiplication is with parentheses. So $(2)(2)$ is 2 *times* 2.

If we plug in $N = 2$ and $x = 3$, then

$N^x = 2^3 = (2)(2)(2) = 8$

If we plug in $N = 2$ and $x = 4$, then

$N^x = 2^4 = (2)(2)(2)(2) = 16$

If you like equations—and who doesn't—the penny-doubled challenge would be represented like this:

Value on Day x = ($0.01)(2)^{(x-1)}$

where 2 represents doubling and $0.01 is a penny, of course.

Value on Day 7 = ($0.01) $(2)^{(7-1)}$ = ($0.01) $(2)^{(6)}$ = $0.64

Value on Day 30 = ($0.01) $(2)^{(30-1)}$ = ($0.01) $(2)^{(29)}$ = $5,368,709.12

If you wanted to know what would happen if you tripled your money, the equation would look like this:

Value on Day x = ($0.01) $(3)^{(x-1)}$

Value on Day 7 = ($0.01) $(3)^{(7-1)}$ = ($0.01) $(3)^{(6)}$ = $7.29

Value on Day 30 = ($0.01) $(3)^{(30-1)}$ = ($0.01) $(3)^{(29)}$ = $686,303,773,648.83

Wow! More than $686 billion! Even Laura Friendly doesn't have that kind of money.

It's also satisfying to view doubling in chart form.

No doubt, a penny doubled is worth the wait.

A Penny Doubled	
Day 1	$0.01
Day 2	$0.02
Day 3	$0.04
Day 4	$0.08
Day 5	$0.16
Day 6	$0.32
Day 7	$0.64
Day 8	$1.28
Day 9	$2.56
Day 10	$5.12
Day 11	$10.24
Day 12	$20.48
Day 13	$40.96
Day 14	$81.92
Day 15	$163.84
Day 16	$327.68
Day 17	$655.36
Day 18	$1,310.72
Day 19	$2,621.44
Day 20	$5,242.88
Day 21	$10,485.76
Day 22	$20,971.52
Day 23	$41,943.04
Day 24	$83,886.08
Day 25	$167,772.16
Day 26	$335,544.32
Day 27	$671,088.64
Day 28	$1,342,177.28
Day 29	$2,684,354.56
Day 30	$5,368,709.12

A 10 Percent Raise

In the story, Felix and Benji pay their driver one thousand dollars on his first day of work and then give him a 10 percent raise each day after that. Ten percent may not sound like a lot, but it *literally* adds up to a substantial amount.

Again, if you like equations—and who doesn't—it would be represented like this.

Value on Day x = \$1,000 $(1 + 0.10)^{(x-1)}$
where \$1,000 is the starting amount and 0.10 is 10% in decimal form ($^{10}/_{100}$ = 0.10).

Value on Day 7 = \$1,000 $(1 + 0.10)^{(7-1)}$ = \$1,771.56

You can substitute values to see how much money can be earned for different situations. For example, try to negotiate your allowance. Perhaps you start at five dollars per week and ask for a weekly increase of 3 percent, assuming you do a good job with your chores.

Value on Week x = \$5 $(1 + 0.03)^{(x-1)}$
where \$5 is the starting amount and 0.03 is 3% in decimal form ($^{3}/_{100}$ = 0.03).

Value on Week 1 = \$5 $(1 + 0.03)^{(1-1)}$ = \$5

Value on Week 10 = \$5 $(1 + 0.03)^{(10\text{-}1)}$ = \$6.52

And after a year:

Value on Week 52 = \$5 $(1 + 0.03)^{(52\text{-}1)}$ = \$22.58

That's some nice dough.

To see the true potential on a compounded raise, compare what a driver would make with no raise versus a daily 10 percent raise over thirty days.

It's a difference of \$134,494.02—a substantial amount indeed.

No Raise vs. 10 Percent Raise		
	$1,000 per day	**$1,000 plus 10%**
Day 1	$1,000.00	$1,000.00
Day 2	$1,000.00	$1,100.00
Day 3	$1,000.00	$1,210.00
Day 4	$1,000.00	$1,331.00
Day 5	$1,000.00	$1,464.10
Day 6	$1,000.00	$1,610.51
Day 7	$1,000.00	$1,771.56
Day 8	$1,000.00	$1,948.72
Day 9	$1,000.00	$2,143.59
Day 10	$1,000.00	$2,357.95
Day 11	$1,000.00	$2,593.74
Day 12	$1,000.00	$2,853.12
Day 13	$1,000.00	$3,138.43
Day 14	$1,000.00	$3,452.27
Day 15	$1,000.00	$3,797.50
Day 16	$1,000.00	$4,177.25
Day 17	$1,000.00	$4,594.97
Day 18	$1,000.00	$5,054.47
Day 19	$1,000.00	$5,559.92
Day 20	$1,000.00	$6,115.91
Day 21	$1,000.00	$6,727.50
Day 22	$1,000.00	$7,400.25
Day 23	$1,000.00	$8,140.27
Day 24	$1,000.00	$8,954.30
Day 25	$1,000.00	$9,849.73
Day 26	$1,000.00	$10,834.71
Day 27	$1,000.00	$11,918.18
Day 28	$1,000.00	$13,109.99
Day 29	$1,000.00	$14,420.99
Day 30	$1,000.00	$15,863.09
	$30,000.00	$164,494.02

Acknowledgments

When it comes to writing support, I'm truly rich. This book would not have been possible without the team of people (and dogs) who assist and encourage me.

Carolyn Coman—my mentor, my friend, and an all-around awesome person—has held my hand through the toughest revisions. My fantastic editor, Caroline Abbey, has been encouraging, thoughtful, and patient every step of the way. And my incredible agent, Lori Kilkelly, puts up with a lot, goes the extra mile, and is responsible for so many of my dreams coming true.

As always, hugs and high fives to the Random House team, including Kathy Dunn, Michelle Nagler, Michelle Cunningham, Barbara Bakowski, Alison Kolani, Kelly McGauley, and Kristin Schulz.

I'm fortunate to have an amazing writing community.

Thanks to my friends in 32 Zoo, Electric Eighteens, LK Literary, and SCBWI-Carolinas. And special appreciation for Laura Gehl, Jason June, Peter McCleery, Anthony Piraino, and Kelly Yang for their input on this book.

The fictitious Max Wade is a character named by the Pearce family—a silent auction prize from Bookmarks. Thank you, Max, Sam, and Marc, for supporting our independent bookstore in Winston-Salem, North Carolina.

And speaking of bookstores, a shout-out to all my supportive North Carolina shops from the coast to the mountains. Thank you, Bookmarks, Scuppernong Books, Wonderland Bookshop, Flyleaf Books, McIntyre's Books, the Country Bookshop, Park Roads Books, Quail Ridge Books, Read with Me, Page 158 Books, Malaprop's Bookstore, and all the other booksellers who are putting books in the hands of young readers.

Thank you to Clemmons Elementary for helping me with "research" on this book. *I told you I'd mention you!*

Finally, I'm able to write books because of the support and encouragement of my friends and family, especially Kristen, Mom, and Dad. Thank you, all! To Cora, Lily, Henry, and Brett: *I love writing, but I love y'all even more. You're the best parts of my life.* And though they can't read, I must mention the McAnulty pack of dogs—Munchkin, Jack, and Reykja. *Woof!*

And for the third time, I'd like to thank Lin-Manuel Miranda. *Your creativity and kindness are inspiring.* (I've acknowledged Lin in each of my previous novels and will continue to acknowledge him until he acknowledges my acknowledgment. Who am I kidding? I'll probably keep doing it after that point too.)